PENGUI

McGA
POLITI

Bartholomew Gill, Irish-American in descent, has received an M. Litt. degree from Trinity College in Dublin and presently lives in New York State. His other novels include *Little Augie's Lament*, *Lucky Shuffles*, *McGarr and the Sienese Conspiracy*, and *McGarr on the Cliffs of Moher*.

McGarr and the Politician's Wife

by Bartholomew Gill

PENGUIN BOOKS

Penguin Books Ltd, Harmondsworth,
Middlesex, England
Penguin Books, 625 Madison Avenue,
New York, New York 10022, U.S.A.
Penguin Books Australia Ltd, Ringwood,
Victoria, Australia
Penguin Books Canada Limited, 2801 John Street,
Markham, Ontario, Canada L3R 1B4
Penguin Books (N.Z.) Ltd, 182–190 Wairau Road,
Auckland 10, New Zealand

First published in the United States of America by
Charles Scribner's Sons 1977
First published in Canada by
Charles Scribner's Sons 1977
Published in Penguin Books 1982

LIBRARY OF CONGRESS CATALOGING IN PUBLICATION DATA
Gill, Bartholomew, 1943–
McGarr and the politician's wife.
Reprint. Originally published: New York: Scribner, c1977.
I. Title.
PS3563.A296M3 1982 813'.54 81-15802
ISBN 0 14 00.5984 9 AACR2

Printed in the United States of America by
George Banta Co., Inc., Harrisonburg, Virginia
Set in CRT Caledonia

McGarr and the Politician's Wife

1

In the twilight near the Killiney Bay Yacht Club, all that flowed was grey. The tidefall, a shimmering rush like molten lead, heeled buoys and made the yachts dance at their moorings. White patches of the houses on the steep hill had begun to mute with dusk. Only the gorse of Bray Head ten miles south caught the last of the sun and bristled green. Between these two promontories, a gentle sweep of ivory beach fringed the valley floor. It wasn't only approaching night that made the wind off the Irish Sea cold. Autumn had arrived.

Chief Inspector of Detectives Peter McGarr remembered Wicklow from the thirties, when, as a lad, his family—all thirteen of them—would board a tram at Inchicore, a train in Dublin, and, debouching at Bray, would climb the Head to Greystones. Then Bray was a resort town, not the sprawling suburb of small homes he could see before him. But the view from Killiney was still more beautiful than any of those his former police travels for Interpol had shown him. He had jumped at the chance to get away from Dublin

Castle. There, even the most trivial item of business involved the politics of the fighting in the North. This case seemed free from that sordid bog and accommodatingly routine

McGarr glanced down at his feet. Here the dock was old. He wondered how it would be to lay his head on a yawing plank and sight down its weathered grooves, white as cigarette ash. This the man just pulled from the water by the club steward and dock boy might have done, had his eyeballs not drifted into his head. His sclerae alone were visible when McGarr depressed a tanned eyelid. His bald head was split to expose a buff wedge of cranium, which, now that the seawater no longer rinsed the wound, quickly filled with a thin vermilion fluid like blood. In spasms, his body pushed brine from his nose and mouth. He was not dead.

"Ah, the poor blighter," said a towering man in a blue Garda uniform. The chin strap of his cap cinched tightly about a flame-red face. "Easy with him, lads. Go easy." The ambulance attendants were lifting the victim onto a stretcher. Superintendent Liam O'Shaughnessy was one of McGarr's assistants, his perennial companion, and good friend. He had yet to accustom himself to the spectacle of others in pain, however, and agonized over every injury.

McGarr said, "Go with him, Liam. See what the hospital can discover." O'Shaughnessy had already searched the man's pockets and the cabin of the vessel, abeam of which the police inquirers now stood. He had found only a small brass key attached to a wooden float. On it a Dublin phone number had been scratched.

The boat was a trim schooner of some sixty feet,

bug-eye rigged, and perhaps the high point of Alden small-schooner design. The low cabin, spoon bow, and graceful lines betrayed this much to McGarr, who, during the late fifties and sixties, had covered Marseilles and as much of the Riviera as was important to large-scale drug traffickers. Thus, he had learned to distinguish between types of pleasure craft, their potential uses and cargo capacities.

This boat, however, was a near wreck, its brightwork weathered grey and blackening with rot in places. The shrouds were rusted, deck caulking heaved, winches appearing to be locked with corrosion. The main hatch cover had been split months past as though a forcible entry had been gained. A halo of charring ringed the perimeter of the aftmost porthole on this, the port side. McGarr speculated that the man, while drunk, had set the galley afire. Also, the mainsail was lying in heaps, blood-spattered, on the cabin roof. In the shadows of a soda-pop case that was set on an edge and read "Canada Dry," an inch of Mt. Gay rum shimmered in a quart bottle. A jelly glass nearby held less.

McGarr asked the dock boy, an ancient man who wore a battered yachting cap, service khakis, and a heavy cardigan through which the elbows of his shirt peeked, "Was this the Yank's port of entry? How much and what sort of cargo did he off-load here? Certainly you required him to log in with the club's commodore—may I see the book, please? How much rum did he drink daily and where did he purchase it? Lastly, how did the accident occur?" The inspector didn't really expect answers. The battery of questions was merely his way of catching the wary off balance: that he knew with one glance the origin of the victim, a good deal about the boat, and something of nautical procedures; that he was fully prepared to ask all the questions should the dock boy or the steward, who now pushed through the other policemen and faced McGarr, prove reticent. Once either of them began speaking, however, McGarr would say as little as possible and simply stare at the speaker, his hazel eyes unblinking and attentive.

The ploy worked, for the eight men on the dock turned to him. McGarr was very short, not reaching, it seemed, shoulder level of the tallest. Even by Dublin standards, McGarr's dress was nondescript—full-length tan raincoat, dark suit, tie, white shirt, and cordovan bluchers polished to a high gloss. Bald, McGarr always wore a hat or cap, depending on the weather. Today it was a brown derby. But for a rather long and bony nose, his features were regular. He perpetually smoked Woodbine thins, puffing on one often enough to keep it lit. In all, he looked like a minor civil servant or a successful racetrack tout. Anonymity, he had found, was the most effective mask in police work.

The steward was a large man with a barrel chest and a full, curly beard, frosting at the tips. This made his protrusive lower lip seem very red and wet. He took one inclusive look at McGarr and then turned his shoulder, which was bulging in a blue blazer with the yacht-club insignia on the pocket. "You see," he said to the other, more official-looking policemen—one from Internal Security, the other from the Dun Laoghaire barracks of the Garda; McGarr and his second assistant, Hughie Ward, comprised the lot—"this was a curious fellow." Like most Englishmen in Ireland, the steward's accent had become hopelessly exaggerated, a drawl more groan than voice. "He would sit here all day long, sipping from that bloody jam jar and staring—" The steward became aware that all the other police were not looking at him but at McGarr. He turned to the inspector—"at that bloody barge."

McGarr said, "You're too kind. Did you find him first?"

"No."

"Did you see the accident happen?"

"No."

"Then if you'll husband your opinions until all of us can give you our individual attentions, we'll be eternally grateful." He took the dock boy by the elbow, and passing by the steward, added, "Jealously, jealously."

McGarr led the old man over the cap rail and onto the afterdeck of the schooner. "What's she called?" he asked in the conspiratorial whisper in which the older generations of Irish prefer to converse.

"*Virelay,* New York."

"What's that mean?"

"He, the poor bastard, says it's a sort of poem, but I'd say, looking about, it's something more like 'Come Back Paddy Riley,' sung in a weak tremolo."

"Smoke?"

"Thank you, sorr. I'm Billy Martin."

"How did it happen?"

Martin bent for McGarr's light. He had a porter nose and McGarr could detect the sweet reek of rum on him. "As you can see from the sail, the winch handle bashed his sconce."

"Did you see it happen?"

"No, sir. I had gone for something"—Martin turned his back to the steward on the dock and confided—"something to cut the stuff with. I don't know how the bloody Yank could drink it all day and all night. Christ, it's hotter than horse piss, and kick! I ducked out to mix mine with Miwadi and water."

"And?"

"And when I got back I heard him thrashing about the water, blowing like a porpoise. I grabbed the boat hook and pulled him alongside. We"—Martin indicated the steward—"pulled the unlucky bugger on board. It was desperate shape he was in."

Glancing up at the hill, McGarr caught the rainbow flash of high-powered glasses and made mental note. "How long were you gone, Billy?"

"Not long. To be honest, it was about quitting time and there was just the wee-est drop left, and rather . . . I hurried back."

"So this"—McGarr pointed to the greening winch handle—"is what did it."

"No question about it, sir. A thin piece of his pate, there"—Martin pointed to a bloody smear between the cranking handle and the lever arm—"proves it. Ah, Jasus, I should've been a cop. Think of the pension I'd have now—medical care, a union to protect me." He shook his head and commiserated with himself for several moments. When he looked up, McGarr was staring at him. "We were raising the sail to dry her, we were. 'Twas the only job the feller would allow to be done on the craft. He'd just get jarred and pop up the mainsail now and again. Apart from that, he sat on that case and smoked and stared."

"Was he broke?"

"Don't know. Could be. But he paid dockage right on time and took a cab to Dublin and back for supplies." Martin jerked a thumb toward the dock and the soda case with the bottle inside. "It's not everywhere you can purchase that stingo, you know.'

"How does this thing work, Billy?"

"Well, you take this lever—" He reached for the winch handle.

McGarr restrained him. "Don't touch it, please, Billy."

"—like so and you crank it until the mainsail is raised. When the slide is so corroded like this, it takes a ton of man to hoist her aloft. Then you slip this holding tooth into the cam and she locks."

McGarr looked up at Martin as though expecting to be further enlightened. So far the old man had told him nothing.

"But if she doesn't hold, the weight of that sail will make the winch spin like a top, and the handle—feel it," Martin again reached for the lever but McGarr restrained him, "—could give a man one hell of a knock. You saw so yourself."

"But how could the holding tooth become disengaged from the cam?"

"Aw, c'mon, McGarr," said Will Hare from Internal Security. "We all know this is a busman's holiday. Let's adjourn to the Khyber Pass"—which was a large hotel between the hills that separated Killiney from Dalkey. "The man got drunk and his finger slipped."

"Was he an experienced seaman?" McGarr asked the old man.

"Fine, I should imagine. The boat plate says she was built in Camden, Maine. The transom says New York. He had the air of a sailor, if you know what I mean."

"Friends here?" McGarr indicated the homes on the hill, the yacht club.

"Not a one, in fact . . ." Martin again glanced over his shoulder at the steward on the dock.

"Could somebody else have seen the accident occur?"

"Nobody. The season is spent. As you can see, things have been so arranged that these two cabin cruisers shield the boat from the observation deck. Maybe owned by somebody who maintained her properly this boat might fit in around here. She's a sweet craft in spite of her condition. But—"

"I understand." McGarr flicked the butt of his Woodbine into the grey water of the Irish Sea. The person who had phoned the authorities had an accent that the switchboard operator said was not exactly Irish. "Who called us?"

"The skipper, I believe. Anyhow, I didn't. I stayed right here and ministered to the gent." Martin again meant the yacht-club steward on the dock.

McGarr's coworkers were impatient, hands in raincoat pockets, staring up at the hill or shifting from foot to foot. "Shall we meet you there?" Hare asked.

"Have one in triplicate for me," said McGarr.

"Inspector?" Hughie Ward asked. He was a black Irishman—curly black hair, black eyes, sallow skin, and white, well-formed teeth. Now in his early thirties, his capacity to attract women seemed as infinite as their power to please him, but in numbers alone. Ward was a confirmed bachelor. On Friday nights, such as this, the Khyber Pass was filled with unattached young women. Since the bomb blast in Dublin two months ago, the pace of Ward's police work had been grueling. McGarr tossed the key they had found in the Yank's pocket to Ward and said, "By Monday." Ward went off with the others.

To the steward on the dock, McGarr said, "Hand me that bottle, would you please, skipper?"

"I beg your pardon." He was a fat man with a frog's build, all his weight up front in his chest and stomach. His hips were very narrow and legs thin. He wore white duck trousers and a blue Trinity rugby shirt.

"The bottle. In the box. Would you hand it to me, please?"

With exaggerated disdain and much effort, the steward bent and pulled the bottle from behind the soda case. Reaching over the cap rail of the schooner, he handed it to the inspector. It was nearly dark, and lights had begun appearing on the hillside.

"Will you join me?" McGarr asked the dock boy.

Martin said to the steward, "It's past time, sorr," took the bottle, and drank. He handed it back to McGarr, who followed suit. The rum was smooth, unlike any McGarr had ever tasted. It pleased him and he took another sip.

"May I go?" the steward asked.

"Just a few moments more, please, *sorr,*" said McGarr. He then offered the bottle to Martin once more. "How do you think he managed to land in the water?"

"In a blind stagger, whether from the booze"—Martin drank—"or the blow. That bites without a chaser." He meant the rum.

McGarr could hear the police car working up the steep grade toward the hotel.

Taking a pocket torch from his raincoat, McGarr stepped down the ladder of the companionway. As he had suspected, the galley area had recently suffered a grease fire that had charred the interior cabin trunk and roof. The port bunk was a nest of funky clothes, marine periodicals, and another half-filled bottle of rum. This McGarr put in the deep pocket of his raincoat. Everything—lockers, head, fo'c'sle—was so damp, mildewy, or actually wet, McGarr speculated the water that filled the bilges was more rain seeping through the deck chinks than hull leakage. As he replaced the floorboards, he noticed how totally they were stained. McGarr ran a corner of his handkerchief over the stained area until a smudge appeared in the cotton.

He then noticed a band of what proved to be the halter top of a woman's bathing suit dangling from a partially open locker. The label read B. Altman, 38C. The starboard lockers were filled with neatly folded women's clothes purchased from smart shops in New York, London, Paris, Curaçao, Barbados, all, however, rank with mildew. Some things—hosiery, underwear, a lilac dress—had decomposed. McGarr failed to find one identifying mark, laundry or personal, on anything. McGarr poised himself, and when swinging the chart locker down from its perch, stepped out of the way. As he had expected, the chart locker had caught a puddle of rain from the leaking deck. The light from the pocket torch glistened on the sodden charts, which stuck together, so that McGarr had to pull one from the others. The Caribbean islands, east coast of the United States and Canada, the North Atlantic, and Ireland were included. In red pencil, a transatlantic route had been traced, giving dates and times of sun sightings. If the map was correct, landfall had been somewhere in Galway fourteen months before. His last bearing would have taken him into Kilronan on the Isle of Inishmore.

Below these charts he found the ship's documents. The title, issued by the U.S. Coast Guard, said one Andrew A. Mucci of Essex, Connecticut, had been the last owner, having purchased the *Virelay* on September 11, 1947. McGarr doubted he was the man who had been lying on the dock, since between '54 and '67 the boat had remained unregistered.

Also, at first McGarr couldn't locate the boat's auxiliary engine. One did not sail such a large boat in the often windless and shoal-draught waters of Long Island Sound without power, much less the often squally Irish Sea. With the pocket torch, he found the engine emplacement bolts and the oil-stained framing pieces behind the companionway ladder, where the engine had been resting not long past. Much of the grease was still glistening.

On deck, he removed the handle from its chock in the winch and wrapped it in his handkerchief. This he carefully slipped in his other raincoat pocket.

Martin had finished the other bottle.

"What is your opinion of the man?"

Martin raised the bottle. "I liked him. I mean, I *like* him."

"Was he married or did he, say, ever have a female companion on board?"

"Him? Never. He was—how shall I put it—a drinking man."

"Thank you." McGarr stepped off the boat. He asked the steward, "How was it that you were so near this boat when the accident happened?"

"I manage the club and your man." He meant Martin.

The booze had made the old man voluble. Stepping off the boat, he muttered, "Feckin' blimp."

McGarr's nostrils widened as he tried to contain a laugh. "I get the feeling you don't care for the Yank."

"In all candor," the steward intoned, eyeing Martin

malevolently as the old man dipped a hard-bristle pushbroom into the water and began scrubbing the blood from thc dock, "I must admit I did not." The gathering clouds parted briefly and a crescent moon flooded the bay with a brilliant, achromatic light. "This *is* a private club. He was flying the burgee of the New York Yacht Club when he put in here, and so we were forced to take him. I don't know why a man such as he with a boat such as that wouldn't prefer to tie up at a breakwater where the dockage is gratis and one's eccentricities are not self-consciously offensive to those who share the facilities."

McGarr furrowed his brow as though not understanding.

The steward explained. "Well, the man gave me the most lugubrious sensation. To tell you the truth, what with his bald head, pug nose, and heavy beard, he reminded me of Jackson Pollock in decline. He not only drank like Pollock—desperately—but also smoked like the man, one cigarette after another—"

McGarr made a show of drawing from his Woodbine.

"—all the while staring at the hulk as though it were some wretched composition of his with which he wouldn't be quite satisfied until it was an utterly insufferable eyesore or foundered."

"Pollock? I thought that was a type of fish," said McGarr, playing the ignorant gumshoe.

The steward glanced at him disdainfully.

"Pompous ass," Martin muttered.

"His name?"

"Ovens."

"First?"

"Something ignoble the like of Bobby."

"Robert?"

"Bob-by, I said."

"And yours?"

"Hubbard."

"First?"

"H. K. C."

"First?"

"Is this really necessary?"

McGarr smiled.

"Horace."

"Address."

"Fitzwilliam Square."

"Dublin?"

"Of course." It was one of the most prestigious addresses in all of Ireland.

McGarr turned to go. He stopped suddenly and pulled the bottle of Mt. Gay from his raincoat. He pried off the cork. "Drink?" he asked Hubbard, who averted his head. "To the Queen," said McGarr.

When he had replaced the bottle in his raincoat, he began to leave, but once more he turned back. "By the by, Horace Hubbard—where were you exactly when Ovens hit the water?"

"On the dock."

"Here"—McGarr pointed to where they were standing, roughly abeam of the schooner—"or there?" He indicated the dock which formed an L and nearly met the bowsprit of the boat.

"There."

"You'll sign a statement to that effect tomorrow?"

"Certainly."

"Good night, Billy," said McGarr.

"G'luck, Inspector," said Martin, as though tossing back a jar in a pub.

At the Khyber Pass, Hughie Ward had engaged the attentions of a nearly beautiful girl. She reminded McGarr of ripe olives and heady red wine from the cask. She had piled her long black hair on the back of her head. Her neck and arms were thin, facial features precise, complexion golden, and eyes deep black. Her short crimson dress, a chemical weave, adhered to her body in tight patches.

"You know," said Ward to the girl, whose name was Sheila Byrne, "you're a wicked woman."

Her hand jumped for her pack of cigarettes. "Oh, really?" McGarr put her at eighteen years, hardly old enough to be in the lounge.

Now storm clouds were racing across Killiney Bay.

"Yes, really. You are." Ward was staring at her fingers, which made her even more nervous.

"Cigarette?" she offered. Her chin was dimpled, cheeks flushed.

"No, thanks."

She offered the pack to McGarr, who showed her he already had one lit.

She placed the cigarette at the corner of her mouth.

Ward took the lighter from her hand, snapped it, and held the flame to the end.

She had just begun to smoke—one eye squinted shut, lips too wet. "*Do* explain."

"Oh, I don't think it needs explaining." With a click, Ward laid the lighter on the glass-top table and allowed his eyes to slide up her thighs. He was animated, his smile full, all his attention concentrated upon her. "It's quite obvious. Why, even the way you offer me a cigarette—there's so much sophistication, so much promise, so much . . . I don't think I can find the right word yet, I mean, at this point in our relationship, but it's there . . . in your eyes." He looked into her eyes, fixing her with his gaze.

She couldn't look away. She pulled a deep drag from the cigarette, held it for a long time—her eyes narrowing in a flicker of candlelight, lips parted slightly in a smile—and exhaled, pushing the smoke through her nostrils so the funnels hit the top of the table and billowed into Ward's face.

McGarr finished his drink and turned his Mini-Cooper back toward Dublin.

It had begun to rain now, and the line of cars fleeing Dublin for the weekend was solid as far as Shankhill, yellow lights reflecting off the wet road as in a blurry mirror.

McGarr dropped off the winch handle at the police laboratory in Kilmainham and fifteen minutes later parked the Cooper in front of his own house, a modest, two-story, brick Victorian, the ivy so entrenched here in Rathmines it stopped the gutters of the house twice yearly. A lamp cast a yellow glow through the parlor curtains. He could see just the top of his reading chair. He switched off the engine and went in to his supper.

Noreen, his wife, had all the advantages of a small person: well-formed limbs and a grace of movement. Her hair was a glossy nest of tight copper curls and her eyes were green. McGarr discussed every aspect of his job with her, and she was scrupulously discreet about the details. "Two for the price of one," a former minister for justice had always joked when introducing them.

McGarr drew the rum bottle from his pocket and said, "First clue."

She was busy preparing supper, now whipping a mousse of fresh strawberries.

"And second, this spot."

"Give us a sniff," she said.

He held the hanky to her nose. "Gun oil."

"Are you sure?"

"Quite."

"Dammit," McGarr said and walked into the pantry to mix himself a rum drink. In the past he had found her sense of smell to be very acute. Also, he had hoped the case would be straight police work, no politics; had hoped Ovens and the *Virelay* weren't involved in anything like gunrunning.

The phone rang. He stepped into the dining room to answer it. Liam O'Shaughnessy said, "The Lord did not grant the poor bugger a quick death. The doctor says he's unconscious and might go into coma. Also, he's debilitated from years of booze. Says it's a miracle he was up and walking around to get clubbed."

"What?"

"Says he couldn't imagine a winch handle on a yacht striking a man three times. Once, perhaps, but unlikely. Twice, most improbable. Thrice, never. Says he had wanted to change his blood but he was too weak."

"What?"

"Die-alley-sis."

"When do they expect him to come around?"

"Doctor says he can't tell yet."

"Where will you be if I need you this—"

"Consider this call having been made from Galway."

"Take care." McGarr decided not to bother O'Shaughnessy about *Virelay*'s arrival in Ireland yet. Sunday would be soon enough. He was a bachelor like Ward and visited his family in the West whenever police business was slack, which now was seldom.

That the force of the winch handle had not killed Ovens, whose sconce was probably paper-thin like other inveterate alcoholics, bothered him. He wondered how even a drunken sailor could allow the holding tooth to slip from the cog wheel, how the top of Ovens' head could have come to be so low as to receive such blows, and finally, how he could have been struck three times. Could somebody have been waiting for him in the companionway and then have slipped out when Martin ministered to him and Hubbard went for help? What reason could either Martin or Hubbard have for wanting to kill the man? Quite obviously, Hubbard didn't care for Ovens, but McGarr believed Hubbard was too smart to botch such a job and would never have chosen that occasion. But McGarr's first impressions had been wrong in the past.

McGarr phoned Internal Security and asked them to rescind the traveling privileges of Horace C. K. Hubbard of Fitzwilliam Square. He then called the Telephone Bureau and asked for the address of the phone number on the key float. The attendant told him he was not at liberty to divulge the address of an unlisted number. McGarr explained who he was, and the man replied testily, "I couldn't care if you were Michael the Archangel descending" and hung up.

Back in the kitchen, Noreen was moving quickly from range top to oven, to icebox, to sink. Most women, he noted, did not know how to use their feet and slapped them down as though they disdained the earth, their buttocks trembling, calf muscles quaking. Noreen, however, had a body so perfectly proportioned, McGarr experienced an actual physical pang of hunger watching the pale green of her dress slide over her hips, her steps precise and decorous.

2

The storm had passed and the morning was brilliant, what McGarr believed to be the last week of good weather before the winter rains set in. He carried his breakfast tea into the living room and sat in the full sun as he leafed through the morning papers. The heat made him lazy and his mind wandered pleasantly. In the distance, a toneless bell was ringing and only audible on the near rock of the cradle when the clapper fell like a hammer onto a boiler plate. Across the cloudless sky, a jet was embossing twin tracks that merged, sank, then disintegrated in hyphens. It was windy and crisp outside.

Thus, McGarr was infused with a feeling of profound well-being when he heard his wife's light feet on the stairs. She was dressed in a heavy fisherman's knit sweater, cream linen shorts to match, and canvas yachting shoes that they had bought while he was on assignment in France.

"What's up?" he asked.

"The near murder of a visitor to the land of a thousand welcomes. I, for one, am going to protect your reputation for doggedness. I've put your boating gear out on the bed and will call the Khyber for a luncheon reservation. Tramping around the hill to locate whoever was using those high-powered glasses should make us good and hungry."

"Are you daft? This is Saturday."

"And well I, who have been cooped up in Rathmines all week, know." Noreen's legs were at once tanned and freckled. The bulky sweater made her seem fuller in the chest.

"It's not as simple as all that. I've got to put certain things in motion first."

"Your backside and what else?"

McGarr stood. Sleep was still upon him and his limbs were stiff. "Well, first this number."

"Give it here."

He took his pen from his shirt pocket and wrote on a corner of the newspaper the phone number they had found on the key float. "And then I've got to send McKeon down to the yacht club to take statements from Martin and Hubbard. And then—it's too damn early and too damn nice to be arsing around with police work."

The phone was only a few feet away and already Noreen was dialing the department. "Hello," she said, "this is Chief Inspector of Detectives Peter McGarr's secretary."

Even from the parlor McGarr could hear the howl.

"Listen, Bernie, this is Noreen. Peter wants you . . ."

McGarr coerced his legs up the stairs to the bedroom. Among the Irish, McGarr thought, it wasn't unusual to marry a younger woman. At that moment, however, the custom seemed to him just another atavism that harked back to an even more barbarous age.

While he was dressing the phone rang. It was Ward, who told Noreen he had located a lock that accepted the key they had found on Ovens.

In his shorts, McGarr took the steps downstairs two at a time. Noreen handed him the receiver. "This soon? What have you got?" McGarr's knees were stubby and pink.

"You know the girl I was with last night at the Khyber? Her father keeps a boat on the breakwater in Dun Laoghaire. That key is to the shower facilities at the boatyard nearby. She recognized it right away."

"Was that Ovens' official port of entry?"

"Don't think so, but *Virelay* was hauled here and the engine removed."

"Where are you now?"

"At the boatyard. I thought you might like to talk to the yard boss. He tells a whopper about Ovens. I've taken him to the Dolphin, since he knocks off at eleven of a Saturday. Do you know the place? I'll stand him a round or two, *if* the department will cover my losses."

"You do a lot of thinking for an under-assistant, a lot of talking, and far too much round-standing whenever there's a hint the expense might be justified. How many are there in your party?"

"Forty-seven. I'll get a receipt."

McGarr hung up. His interest was now thoroughly aroused. Noreen had gotten no answer from the telephone number on the key float.

All Ireland, it seemed, was marketing in Dublin today. The streets were jammed, sidewalk vendors hawking produce at bargain prices. The crops were definitely bumper; all summer the weather had been glorious.

Noreen couldn't find even a taxi stand that a vehicle with a police pass might occupy and finally got caught in a snarl opposite Moore Street. McGarr hopped out and jogged through the milling crowds until, near the corner of O'Connell Street, he was able to nip in a side door of the General Post Office.

Out on the street, McGarr had been an object of great interest to the passersby, even the shabbiest of whom was dressed, Dublin fashion, in conservative attire, but in the GPO he became an excuse for the civil servants there to stop work and strike up a conversation that would surely last ten minutes. His heavy white sweater was slightly large for him and tended to ride over his buttocks. His Bermuda shorts emphasized the girth of his shanks. Finally, without a hat, his bald and nearly pink head, curly red temples, and plain face were unrecognizable to Fran Wilder, who, when he saw this oddity in white approaching him, pretended to busy himself in one of the many thick phone directories that surrounded him. Wilder had the communications registries of the world at his fingertips.

"Francie, may I speak with you a moment?" said McGarr. They had grown up together in Inchicore.

Wilder didn't stir from a squinting perusal of the thick books.

"Francie, it's Peter McGarr."

Wilder looked up. He had a narrow face with a long, bony nose. Close-cropped sideburns and a veritable spray of dark hair on the top of his head made him look like an extinct flightless fowl. "It is?" From staring into phone books half his life, Wilder was myopic. His head turned haltingly as he scanned the switchboards and work area of the busy phone system. He was squinting and blinking. "Where is he?"

"Here, Francie. I'm McGarr."

Wilder's head snapped toward him, and he minutely examined every aspect of the inspector's garb. "So it is, and there for a moment I thought you was a painted Willy. With legs like that I'd be ashamed to walk the streets. Sure and if the fireplugs in Dublin was white, you'd get pissed on for sure."

Wilder told McGarr the number was listed as that for flat 5A, 17 Percy Place, which was a posh address in Ballsbridge.

Like many in Dublin, the street was a row of eighteenth-century brick houses with long flights of stairs to the second floors. McGarr knew that the porter lived on the ground floor, his door under the stairs, that a garden in back ran to an alley and garages. Begonias in green window boxes lined the porter's windows. The Grand Canal was across the street.

"Inspector Peter McGarr and wife, Noreen," McGarr said to an old woman. But for the flower print of her blue dress and thick black shoes, she was wrapped in a grey shawl. "May I ask you a few questions?"

"You may, not that I promise I'll answer. Give that here." The woman meant his badge, which he handed her. From under the shawl she retrieved a pair of thick bifocals with yellowing frames that hung on a black band around her neck.

"McGarr," she said. "Such an odd name."

"Flat five A. May I inquire who leases it?"

"You may until you're blue in the face, but I don't know. Won't you come in." She stood aside, and Noreen and McGarr stepped into her sitting room, from which a small paraffin heater was chasing the dampness of the night's storm. Even its dull blue flame was cheering in the dim interior of the room.

"The monthlies arrive in the form of cashier's checks, so they tell me. But you'll have to get that information from the property owner, whose lawyer manages the finances of the building."

"His name?"

"Greaney on Leeson Street. I don't believe I've seen the occupants more than a dozen times in the past two years. That's how long they've rented the flat out. Traveling people, I assume they are."

"They?" Noreen asked.

"A man and woman. Husband and wife I should think."

"Age?"

"Not young, not old. He's aging some, balding like your man."

"And she?"

"A pretty woman like yourself."

"Ah, thank you, luv," said Noreen, preening self-consciously.

" 'Tis only the truth. There's a noticeable difference in your ages. Have you any wee ones?"

The McGarrs had none by choice, which was a subject more controversial in Ireland than the political disposition of the Six Counties.

"May we see the apartment?" McGarr asked.

"Have you a writ?"

The old lady's knowledge of the law surprised McGarr. He examined her closely. Once handsome, her skin had grown dark with age and now hung on her face in creases and folds. Her blue eyes were still clear, however, and her teeth were her own. Braided hair, snow white, had been piled on top of her head.

She was taller than he and once possessed a full figure, her ankles narrow nonetheless. "What did you say your name was?" he asked as she reached toward a ledge on which the flat keys of the house lay.

"I didn't, Inspector. Megan will do."

"Well, certainly the people who lease the apartment must receive mail and an occasional visitor. What's the name on the postal address?"

"Five A. That's all I've ever seen. If they have visitors, they answer the door themselves. I've got enough to do without playing parlormaid to the tenants."

They followed her up dingy back stairs from which a low door opened onto as bright and airy a foyer as Dublin possessed. McGarr's yachting shoes scuffed on the deep plush of the beige rug. Walls to match held portraits in oil of sundry Irish historical figures. A tasteful chandelier of cut glass illuminated the landing on the third floor. "How much is the rent of five A?" Noreen asked, as they ascended.

"Twenty-nine per."

"Month?" McGarr asked.

The old lady turned to him with a thin smile on her lips. "No, lad—per *week.*"

The apartment was no less agreeable than the hall. Immediately the porch attracted them. Sliding glass doors opened onto its rows of potted plants. McGarr peered over the railing and looked down upon the garden below, which, having thrived through an abnormally sunny summer, now fructified with such abandon that even he detected the aromas of apples, pears, and many flowers just past prime. The mélange was heady to his senses.

The rooms contained simple but expensive furnishings in a style that McGarr called Continental, this is to say, that which Irish and British intellectuals might choose for their flats: bean-bag chairs, Plexiglas tables, circular fluorescent lights that craned from weighted bases and lit half the room. No one motif was dominant, each piece seeming to have been chosen for itself, but all was tasteful. The place was spotless and comfortable, yet strangely its ambience seemed sterile. Certainly, it had not been lived in recently.

While Noreen admired the curious decor, McGarr examined the kitchen cabinets, finding only some tins of foodstuffs and a well-stocked liquor cabinet that contained a half case of Mt. Gay rum. The fridge was empty and switched off, the door slightly ajar.

Meanwhile, the old lady kept up a monologue. "The place gets done out thoroughly once a week no matter how long they're away. The heat goes on come-day-go-day."

That was when McGarr noticed the self-contained central heating system with which the apartment was equipped. It was composed of baseboard electrical units that operated at enormous expense in Ireland.

"I sometimes bring my knitting up here when I water the plants what have a better life than half the poor of this city. I sit here"—she indicated a low couch of at least ten feet—"if only to allay such terrible waste. Every once in a while, when the house is empty, I hear the phone go off. It rang so long three weeks ago I finally climbed all the way up here only to have the operator tell me the call was from Rome. I speak English alone and a smattering of the mother tongue. So much more the shame."

Presently, McGarr was opening bureau drawers in the bedroom and carefully turning back the clothes.

He had not found one written item, picture, or memento. He lingered for some time in the drawer that contained the woman's underthings.

Finally, the old woman said, "I should think such fluff would grow on a man in your profession, Inspector."

Noreen added, "He's beginning to act like one of those, so to speak."

"Ah, there's many a man with a worse failing. The whole country would be better off if the men kept their hands to themselves."

McGarr smiled wanly and walked out of the apartment. That made twice today his sexuality had been questioned. In spite of these insinuations, however, he had noticed that the female occupant of the apartment had a doubtless pleasing bust size of 38C and purchased her clothes at B. Altman and the other shops that figured as the origin of the clothes on the boat. As well, the wardrobe was large, the woman obviously shapely and chic. What troubled McGarr was how a man of Ovens' rough-and-tumble demeanor might fit into this scene. The only men's shoes in the closet were a pair of Topsiders, the American boating moccasin.

The Dolphin was a working-class pub near the Dun Laoghaire docks. Today, the frosted glass door had been jammed open, and the crowd within had spilled onto the street. In spite of the sun and mild weather, all the men wore heavy raincoats and, even when nearly threadbare, a coat and tie below. Several old men scuttled from the bar to the turf accountant's shop next door. As Noreen parked the car, the inspector remembered this was a race day in Britain, the steeplechase in particular.

The interior of the pub was a fug of tobacco smoke, damp clothes, the sweet reek of constantly draining porter taps, and a din almost palpable. Most of the men, arguing in groups over race bets, hushed noticeably as Noreen and McGarr pushed by them.

McGarr thought it was because many recognized him. He was wrong.

"Hey, mister," said one. "You've got a tear in your britches."

McGarr stopped and twisted around to check.

"From the knees down," the old man added, then popped open his toothless jaw and laughed, his friends echoing his mirth.

"What's a stumpy runt like him doing with a handsome, sporting woman like her?" McGarr heard another ask.

"Hold your tongues. That's Peter McGarr, the detective."

"I don't care who he is. He's in *our* bar now and should dress appropriately."

Livid, McGarr squeezed into the seat of the snug beside Sheila Byrne. Most of the patrons were now chuckling, looking back at McGarr and shaking their heads.

"Mornin'," he said to the pretty young woman.

Noreen, Ward, and a man who introduced himself as Brud Clare comprised their party.

"Never mind them, Inspector," said Sheila, pulling his arm to her chest, "I think you look . . . dashing."

Ward couldn't help himself now, and shielding his face behind Clare's shoulder, began a stifled laugh that made the others smirk.

"Watch it, boyo," said McGarr, "or you'll find yourself tracking vagrant tinkers in Donegal."

"Mr. Clare," said Noreen.

"Brud."

"What can you tell us about Bobby Ovens and the *Virelay?*"

The old man who had made the first comment about McGarr's shorts was still staring over at them, his eyes twinkling. His jaw swirled as he worked a plug of chewing tobacco. When McGarr looked up at him, he nudged a companion and began laughing again.

Hughie Ward had made sure the boatyard boss was well into his cups by the time the McGarrs arrived, and Clare was now voluble. "Not one whole hell of a lot. The facts are these." He straightened up and blinked his watering eyes. He was a small man whose calloused hand—the nails black with caulking pitch—bent around his porter glass like a casting. A lit cigarette bristled from between the first two fingers. Above the bar, the television announcer began listing the race entrants. Clare kept his eyes on the box while he spoke.

"He came into the yard about thirteen months ago. The engine of the boat was blown, shrouds busted, had a leak only a man with a strong right arm might contain. Sailed her right into the ways single-handed and doused sail." He leaned over the table so he could talk past Ward and Sheila Byrne. "That's a lot of boat for one man.

"It seems—now and I'm only specalatin', you know—he sailed her from someplace on the other side. I say this because everything he owned was manufactured over there."

"You mean Canada or the United States?" McGarr said, if only to show the others he wasn't still outraged.

Clare blinked once, pulled on his cigarette, and redirected his gaze to the screen. "The engine itself is the strangest case I've run up against in forty-two years at the yard. It sprung an oil leak while he was motoring in a calm not far from Galway. Again, I say this not because Ovens told me so, but because I've seen his charts—"

"Which have a transatlantic route that ends on the Isle of Inishmore."

Eyes still on the screen, Clare twisted his head to one side, which is a sign of concurrence in the Dublin area.

McGarr had become aware of Sheila Byrne's taut breast on his arm. He turned to her and she smiled at him. His wife, however, noticed this, and when he glanced at her, she too smiled, but wryly, and looked up at the horses that were jogging through the paddock and onto the track.

"Most sailors would have despaired. It was the late spring and the western coast of this country is treacherous. Somehow, the man had a store of graphite lubricant aboard, which, after he fixed the oil leak, he melted down, mixed with whatever motor oil he had left, and poured into the crankcase of the ship's diesel. You see, as long as he kept the engine hot, the graphite wouldn't seize. Have you seen the galley?"

McGarr nodded, now realizing that the charring had resulted from no ordinary grease fire.

Noreen was exulting. She had been right; graphite was the base of some types of gun oil.

"Eventually, his fuel ran out. I've got the engine in the yard, if you'd care to look."

The horses had begun lining up for the race.

"What sort of man is he?"

"Different, entirely," said Clare. "He put the boat in with me and asked us to work on it whenever the press of other yard business wasn't severe. That's just the sort of job we like—keeps the crew busy, the yard making money. Everything he wanted done, a complete fitting out. When the big boss asked him if he could pay, the man said, 'I'll pay you. It may take time, but you'll get your money,' in such a way we believed him. I was there, I heard him. That man doesn't say much, so that when he does, it's got punch."

With a shout that caused all the bar patrons to look up, the horses got off.

Clare had to raise his voice and speak directly to McGarr. "And so sometimes when we *were* slack, we had a full gang of men, maybe a half dozen or more, working on that boat. Because the law keeps an alien from working a job that an Irishman might take, the bloke was prohibited from working along with us. He sold his compasses, sextant, and binoculars and rented a garage on Loretto Avenue, about a quarter mile from here. Using whatever scrap lumber he could scrounge and some old tools, he began making furniture, beautiful stuff that sold to all the nobs in Ballsbridge as quickly as he could produce it. It was miraculous what he could knock up from nothing. Often we'd take a couple dozen bottles of stout over to his spot after closing and he'd still be working away."

"Did he drink heavily?" McGarr asked.

The horses had completed a half lap and the bar crowd was roaring at the screen. Clare cupped a hand to his ear.

"Drink?" McGarr repeated.

"I've got one, thanks."

"No—*Ovens* drink?"

"Rum," said Clare, "but not then. It wasn't until later he started hitting it early in the day. Before that he was steady, and for a short time almost managed to keep pace with the work on the ship."

"Did he have a wo-man?" McGarr enunciated precisely.

Several men standing near their table turned and looked at him, then at Sheila and Noreen, who winked. One man raised an eyebrow and turned back to the screen. Horses were serious business in the Dolphin, which no woman or the mention of her should breach.

"I'm coming to that. None of us thought so at first, and one man tried to fix him up with his sister, you know, home to dinner and all that. About the time we had repaired the hull, applied bottom paint, and refloated her, two things happened that changed him completely. Ovens was then way behind, over a thousand pounds, on his payments. First, on a Friday afternoon a big Mercedes pulled into the yard so fast it must have slid ten feet when the woman at the wheel hit the brakes. She got out, ran up to him, and he took her behind a boat where we could hear her talking to him in a loud voice. He got in the car and drove off with her.

"Next morning, a Saturday like this, she returned. I was the only boss on the job. She wanted to know if *Virelay* was fit to sail. I said she was fit but not right, if you know what I mean. She was still a mess and the engine had yet to be overhauled. We were waiting for parts from the Caterpillar company, an outfit from the States."

Two men pushed themselves closest to the television and began hitting the bar, calling out the name Spindrift.

"She then asked to see the boat's account, which I

told her I could not do since it was a private business matter between the yard and Bobby Ovens. To be honest, she was a lovely-looking woman and her smile had a special plea in it. But when she said she wanted to pay the balance, that was another matter altogether —if we could collect ten shillings on the pound for every debt that's owed us, we could pay our own bills —and so I showed her the tab.

"She opened her purse and paid over seventeen hundred pounds in notes so crisp I thought they was counterfeit. She asked me to estimate how much the rest of the work would cost, and I said that much again. Once more she divvied out the sum without batting an eye. Then she asked me if I knew who she was. I had seen her face, mind you, but couldn't decide on where.

"She slapped a hundred pounds on the desk to help me forget and walked out."

"What did she look like?" asked McGarr.

"I forget."

"We could take you downtown, you know."

"I know, but you won't."

"Don't be so sure."

"Tall, small, heavy?" Noreen asked.

"Suffice it to say she was—present company excepted, of course—probably the prettiest woman in all of Ireland, although I'm not sure to this day she's Irish."

The horses had just entered the third lap of the race, and the shouts and curses were dizzying.

Clare continued. "But the strangest thing happened when Ovens found out. When the big boss told him of his fortune, it was like somebody stole his spunk. He stood there dazed, then asked where a good grog shop might be. That's when he started on the rum. He wouldn't let us tighten a spring line on the ship in a storm, just mooned over the thing like it was dying and there was nothing nobody could do. After a while, the boss got sick of seeing him, paid him off the credit balance, and asked him to clear out, which he did in the neatest bit of sailing I've ever seen. He tacked back and forth through the fleet of prams and sailing dinghies, against both wind and tide, then eased off and ran her south with the wind.

"Later, I saw her docked at the Killiney Bay Yacht Club, and him on the dock, staring at the boat in that same dazed way, you know."

"Which garage is it on Loretto Avenue?" McGarr asked.

Suddenly, in the stretch of the final lap, the lead horse fell after vaulting a hurdle. The contenders, right behind, also stumbled, and the bar crowd hushed so totally the silence seemed louder than the former uproar.

"Third garage on the right. Wooden frame, white, and kind of tumbledown," said Clare in an ordinary tone that was audible throughout the bar.

McGarr thanked Clare.

The TV announcer said, "And there, near the edge of the track, is number thirty-one—let me check my roster—" That horse, way on the margin of the hurdle, jumped clear of the pile-up and surged into the lead. "Fine Haven, a dark horse if there ever was one at fifty-six to one."

Standing, McGarr shouted, "Come on, Fine Haven!"

The entire crowd turned to him as he and Noreen left. McGarr knew some of these men had wagered as much as a week's earnings on this race. "And what are *you* drinking tomorrow, Paddy?" he said to the old man who had made fun of his short pants.

Using the phone in the turf accountant's shop next door, McGarr asked the desk sergeant at the Dun Laoghaire Garda barracks to seal the garage that Ovens had used as his work shed. He also asked the Garda to keep an eye on the place.

But on the dock of the Killiney Bay Yacht Club, where weekend boaters were toting gear and supplies aboard their yachts in anticipation of perhaps the last fine weather of the season, McGarr felt very conspicuous. "Count it the last time I'll attempt to dress out of character in *this* country," he said to Noreen.

The yacht-club members seemed comfortable in their clothes. None of the men wore shorts, certainly not a fisherman's sweater, nor the canvas boating shoes the McGarrs had on. Also, most of them were tanned, or even if fair, at least burnt. Gardening in the backyard and a daily round of tennis had given Noreen a delicate tan, but McGarr, whose work kept him in his office or in pubs or trains or automobiles or indoors, was as pallid as only a red-haired Celt can be.

Hubbard, the steward, didn't conceal his mirth as McGarr approached. "Disguised today, I see."

That small statement browned-off the inspector. The jibes of the bar crowd in a working-class pub he could tolerate, but it was not the same from a self-conscious snob like Hubbard. This man wanted to make him feel uncomfortable and out of his depth. Secure in his image as chief inspector of detectives as he had been yesterday, McGarr might have suffered the criticism of a dozen Hubbards, but today he felt like a clown, mucking about in a getup more suited to a beer party in somebody's backyard than the docks of this yacht club. Noreen pulled on his arm as though wanting an introduction.

McGarr said, "I never asked you if Ovens has a lady friend."

"Not all of us are so fortunate." Hubbard touched the peak of his yachting cap and smiled at Noreen.

"Well?"

"Well, what?"

"Has he?"

"Of course not. The man was something of a wretch. Interesting to a jaded sensibility, I should think." He smiled at McGarr as though retasting his breakfast. "But, you know, he was rather raw." Hubbard retained that most damnably superior smile and made it appear he was talking more to Noreen than the inspector.

A cabin cruiser, made heavy with a large party on its afterdeck, hooted twice to the club launch, which piped back. The glare off the water made Noreen shield her eyes with her hand. McGarr had begun to swelter. There wasn't the hint of a breeze in the lee of the clubhouse.

"Did you ever hear him speak of a woman?"

"As I told you yesterday, I didn't *speak* to the man beyond the business of collecting our dock fees."

"Did he claim an Irish address?"

"He didn't claim any address."

"Did you ever see him talk to anybody?"

"If I did, I took no notice."

"How long was he here?"

"Regrettably, two full months and running." Hubbard pointed toward *Virelay,* where a group of people on the dock were examining the bloody sails and afterdeck.

At that moment, Billy Martin passed, saying, "Good morning, sorr. I mean you, Inspector, of course."

Hubbard said, "I thought I told you to clean up that mess or ferry that blasted barge out to a mooring where it will be less of a sideshow."

"By your leave?" Martin asked McGarr, and then explained to Hubbard, "The law *is* the law, sir. This morning's *Independent* says foul play is not yet ruled out in the investigation of Mr. Ovens' injuries." A tightly rolled newspaper stuck from Martin's back pocket.

"Not just yet, please, Billy. I'd like to take another look." McGarr felt he had missed something yesterday and perhaps on the boat. The afternoon had been too balmy, or the feeling in his Dublin Castle office too relaxed, or the prospect of a brief, routine investigation on Killiney Bay followed by an excursion to the Khyber Pass so inviting that McGarr hadn't gathered every essential detail. Maybe the feeling was just the unease his present garb gave him, or maybe the fact that the eccentric Ovens had now become something of an enigma about whom he desired to learn more. In any case, he had ruled out the possibility that the injury was accidental. The doctor's opinion coupled with the mystery of the woman who had paid Ovens' yard bill had set McGarr's suspicions on edge. Something was not quite right here at the scene of the attack, and McGarr knew not what.

As McGarr was ambling off toward the boat, the steward said, "I'm Horace C. K. Hubbard, Mrs. McGarr. Very nice to meet you even under such strained circumstances." He meant McGarr's presence and not the injury that had befallen Ovens.

The inspector turned suddenly and started back on Hubbard. "Let me give you an earful, bucko. A felony has been committed here and twenty-eight years of experience dealing with gobshites like you tells me you're a part of it. Don't leave the country. I've already rescinded your traveling privileges by ordinary transport. Extradition requests to *your* country are quite routine these days."

"Is that a threat? Let me remind you that I am as much an Irishman as you."

"You are like hell! And if a learned opinion can be considered a threat, then you've been threatened."

But aboard the *Virelay,* McGarr could find nothing new. He asked Billy Martin, as he helped the old man furl the blood-stained mainsail, "Where did Hubbard come from when you found Ovens? From the dock, or maybe the cabin?"

"To tell you the truth, he could have come from Mars, for all I know. I was so busy trying to keep the bugger's head out of the water that the first I knew of Hubbard he was at my side reaching for Ovens' shoulders. By the way, how is the poor fellow?"

"Is Hubbard married?"

"No, sir."

"Girl?"

"I think so, although the woman I saw him with could be his sister."

"Pretty?"

"I really didn't notice, but judging from the man himself, if it's his sister, I wouldn't think so."

Noreen, after rummaging through the starboard lockers of *Virelay,* speculated that Ovens' women were one and the same. Whoever she was, she had a spectacular figure and dressed well.

By the time they reached the level at which McGarr judged the flash of the high-powered lens to have originated, the day was torrid. McGarr seized upon this excuse to doff the hated sweater. He really hadn't wanted to continue. An iced drink at the Khyber Pass lounge bar was all he required, and he was regretting having popped off at Hubbard. Noreen urged him on, saying that the view of Killiney Bay from the hill was so spectacular that at any moment some one person was usually scanning the shore with glasses. She was right, and it would be better to contact any such person as soon after the incident as possible.

Noreen took the houses on the high side of the road, McGarr those on the low. He gave her his shield while he kept his identity card.

The first house McGarr approached had a spiked iron fence and a Doberman guard dog with fangs that arced into its mouth like those of a shark. McGarr rang the bell at the gate, but nobody answered and each peal only set off a cascade of savage barking and growling from the dog. In three spots the dog had been prevented from tunneling under the fence by strands of barbed wire. Judiciously McGarr moved on.

In the doorway of the second house, a young mother with one child in her arms, two others clutching her skirts, told him she had so much to do she seldom looked at the bay, much less through high-powered glasses. In the next house, a retired barrister, whom McGarr remembered vaguely from his early days with the Garda, now had cataracts. An Irish-American industrialist and a London-based architect owned the next properties and neither had been in the country yesterday, so said the young man who cared for their gardens. He had gone fishing and wondered if McGarr liked whiting.

While the gardener wrapped the five thin hake in a newspaper at the back of his open van, McGarr glanced out to sea. Banks of purple clouds with towering buff thunderheads fringed the green water and whitecaps to the north. A wet wind had begun to rustle the foliage at roadside. The contrast between the still-brilliant sun on shore and the glowering horizon was startling.

The two houses following were similarly unavailing. One did have a telescope on the porch, but the woman assured the inspector it was an antique that was never used. The second woman was on the telephone. When McGarr climbed the walkway, opened the gate between two clumps of rounded hedges, the breeze running before the approaching storm was blustery, and through it he thought he heard Noreen call his name. Looking down the road he couldn't see her, but again he heard her call.

She was at least a hundred yards above the road, standing near a small white cottage that had been tucked under a ledge of the hill. By the time he reached the narrow lawn, the rain had begun to fall in thick drops that splatted on the flagstone walkway and the slate roof of the cottage. A view of Killiney Bay as fine as that which the Khyber Pass itself enjoyed now presented itself to them. From a central bolt of lightning, seven jagged fingers crimped seaward, a crackling rip of thunder following. They could see the wall of rain rushing over the waves shoreward. Below them on the docks of the Killiney Yacht Club, boat hatches were being rammed shut and several people had begun sprinting toward the clubhouse.

Noreen explained, as they stepped into the cottage, "Mr. Moran's a retired sea captain."

"Tugboats!" a voice from the kitchen corrected.

Two bay windows opened the room to the horizon, sea and sky. A large pair of binoculars sat on a tripod. McGarr put his eyes to the lenses and looked right onto the porch of the yacht club as though he were drinking tea and complaining about the rotten change in the weather among the members. McGarr straightened up.

Here in the cottage a turf fire sputtered in the hearth, and the mantel held a collection of ships in bottles. McGarr could hear the hiss of gas, the pop of a match, and then the sound of tap water plashing into a pot. McGarr noticed the tiles of the room were marked by rubber tires.

A wheelchair appeared in the open kitchen door. It contained an old man with a thick, powerful torso and a grey blanket draped over thin legs. He wore a wool shirt, pale blue. His face was clean-shaven and as smooth as that of a younger man. His shock of white hair had been combed precisely over one temple, the hair part-perfect. He held out his hand. "Walter Moran."

"Peter McGarr."

"Your wife tells me you're from the Castle."

"Inspector of detectives."

"*Chief* inspector," Noreen corrected, proudly.

"I offered Noreen tea. Would you care for something stronger?"

"That I would."

Moran pulled himself over to a low cabinet near one of the windows, and, playing one wheel against the other, swiveled neatly in front of the door. As he reached below and extracted a bottle of sour-mash whiskey, a gust of wind pushed the heavy rain against the glass and blurred the storm scene outside. Thunder sounded in the distance. He placed two tumblers with thick bases on his lap and returned to the hearthside. "Please sit down." He indicated the armchairs to either side, one of which contained a dozing cat. "Just put Jack out. He gets to thinking he's not feline, our living here alone." He poured two stiff drinks and handed one to McGarr. The flame drummed on the bottom of the kettle. "You're here about the trouble at the club yesterday, your wife tells me."

"Yes. I see your glasses are trained on the porch."

"I'm a member of the club," Moran explained in an accent McGarr assessed as only slightly Irish, that of a man who had passed most of his life out of the country. Every available space on the interior wall was covered with watercolors of tugs that bore the Moran name or framed photographs of tugboat scenes. "But I don't want to be a bother all the time, so I attend most functions incognito, so to speak."

"Yesterday, around five-fifteen in the afternoon, were you on the glasses?"

"Sliance!" Moran raised the tumbler, then tossed off the entire drink. He then said, "A little before and a little after."

"Good luck." McGarr drank his down. "It's the little after that that interests me."

Pouring two more drinks, Moran said, "There I can't help you much. I just glanced down and saw the three of them talking near the gate to the slip. Later, when I put my eyes to the glasses, Ovens was in the water, Martin was scrambling around the deck of the boat."

"In any way did the accident appear unusual?"

"I didn't see it happen, mind you, but from the first Martin was looking for the boat hook and Hubbard was running toward the boat."

"It was you who called in the report, wasn't it?"

"Yes. I also sounded this siren." Moran pointed to a switch on the wall near the chair in which Noreen had been sitting. "I won't do so now, since I wouldn't want to be accused of crying wolf. Because I spend so much of my time on the glasses, the Killiney search-and-rescue squad has given me the dubious privilege of sounding this horn from time to time. My neighbors, needless to say, were annoyed. But . . ."

McGarr sipped from the second glass. He wondered why neither Hubbard nor Martin had told him about the siren. It could be that in the confusion they hadn't heard the thing; it could be, however, that either or both of them did not want McGarr to talk to Moran. "How do you know his name?"

"I've sailed with the man and his misfortune is common knowledge." Moran pointed to the morning paper that lay on the table between them. "He was and, I hope, still is . . ." his voice trailed off wistfully as he glanced out at the storm that was frothing the waves of the bay, "a sailor of no mean ability."

"I was told he never sailed the *Virelay* from the day he put in at the yacht club," Noreen said from the kitchen.

"Not on *Virelay*. What he wasn't doing with that vessel was a crime for which at times I couldn't forgive him. Then, at others, say race week this year, I could forgive him high treason."

McGarr raised an eyebrow.

"He stole their thunder, all those fair-weather skippers! Halfway through the race a storm blew up like now. Some of the others reefed, doused sail, and motored, some even heaved sea anchors, but every last one of them but Ovens knuckled under. The boats were one-tonners, fiber glass, tender, light-air craft. Ovens set a new course record.

"Then there was the race last Sunday right here in the bay. Internationals, they were manning. That's the class the youngsters here learn on, all those sailing dinghies you can see moored on the far side of the club. Ovens played a long shot, cutting the final marker close with his boom to starboard on the off chance the other boats, which were running a wind two points off the port quarter, couldn't jibe and beat him to the can. They had right-of-way, but he stole their air, headed up, and put a couple hundred feet between him and the next contender. Afterwards—complaints. They called him a ringer. One member disclosed that Ovens had crewed aboard *Intrepid*. They pissed, they moaned. It was frightful, but he showed them what sailing is all about and in their waters, too. I loved every moment of it.

"Ovens and I, you see," Moran confided, pulling his wallet from his shirt pocket, "are the only two real seamen at the club." He handed his merchant mariner's master's license to McGarr. "Ovens has one also. The rest of them talk like Salty Brine and sail about as well as a kid with a toy boat in Phoenix Park pond."

"Hubbard would have us believe the man had no friends."

"I'm not exactly a friend, but you certainly could call me an admirer. There are two sorts of seamen, you see." Moran mused into the whiskey tumbler. "Gabbers like me, and loners like Ovens. And then there's his girl."

Noreen appeared in the kitchen door.

McGarr put down his glass.

"She crewed for him race week, although, if the truth were known, I'd bet the boat was hers. In little ways some people give away their origins. She has a smile. It's permanent, as though there's some little secret she knows that none of the rest of us mere mortals can."

Noreen said, "That she was born with a fortune which would make a Croesus gag with envy, no doubt." She pushed a tea cart into the room.

"Perhaps," said Moran. "But apart from that she seems pleasant enough in her own way. Her name is Lea. The last I don't know. I remained in the galley the entire voyage."

"Race week?" McGarr asked. "What if the boat—"

"What if the sky should fall? My arms are strong. I could tread water all night."

"Is she, this Lea . . ." McGarr motioned a hand in front of his chest.

"All that and more. But, alas, she knows it, which detracts enormously from her beauty, at least in my eyes. Her manner is—how shall I word it?—overweaning in subtle ways. There's a certain something that mars her beauty and it isn't physical."

"How old is she?"

"That's hard to tell. Thirties, even forties. She's one of those people who seem ageless. I should imagine that even when she was as young as Noreen she looked substantially as she does now. Nearly as handsome as your wife, Peter."

"Tea?" Noreen asked the men to dispel her embarrassment.

Both nodded. "Know anything else about her?" McGarr asked. "Where does she live?"

"Dublin, I believe. She mentioned a David as though he were an obligation, and after the race, when Ovens got drunk, they went aboard *Virelay* and had a row."

"About what?"

"I was in the club. I only saw her leave in a huff, and he never returned to the party to claim the trophy."

An hour later, as Noreen and McGarr were about to leave, Moran added, "Did I tell you I've seen her more recently?"

"Who?"

"Lea."

"Where?"

"Talking to Hubbard on the veranda of the club."

"Is he a sailing man?" Noreen asked.

"The second best, but second by much."

"Are she and Hubbard . . . ?"

"Close? It would appear to me that in some way she's close to every man. During the race she popped her head down the companionway and smiled—well, bared her teeth is more like it—in a way that invited all sorts of untoward imaginings. She was showing ever so little tongue between the edges of her dentition. I could be wrong; the invitation could have been to friendship."

"But then again," said McGarr, "it could have been to pleasure."

"Of that I was very sure."

The McGarrs thanked Moran and left.

Tramping down the hill neither Noreen nor McGarr spoke. Both were thinking. This much they knew: *Virelay* had probably been used to smuggle arms into the country; Hubbard and Martin had not told McGarr the whole story about either the siren or the woman who had been present at the time of the Ovens injury; Hubbard had felt a sort of rivalry existed between him and Ovens. About the woman they knew only that she was wealthy, beautiful, and sometimes lived with Ovens. A man named David could figure in her life too. All things considered, McGarr now believed Ovens' injury had not been accidental.

As Noreen opened the driver-side door of the Cooper, she said, "Shall we skip the Khyber for today? Perhaps we can catch a quick bite on the way to the hospital."

McGarr nodded as he slipped the whiting into the trunk.

There the sister on duty told them Ovens had just regained consciousness. He was in the mercy ward, a long room lined with tall hospital beds made of iron tubing painted grey. Men in every physical state from moribund to nearly well shared this room. Worried families were cramped onto tiny, straight-back chairs around the beds of dying relatives, while near the solarium three men in robes smoked and talked jocularly. Old and young were here, bottles siphoning liquid into the veins of some, a portable television with earphones playing to others. Two men had pushed their beds together and were rolling dice on a game board.

Ovens' entire head was swathed in layers of gauze bandages, but his eyes were open. The doctor, O'Higgins by name, wasn't more than twenty-five, and his profession still regaled him. He said, "Your man was lucky. If the weapon had hit him a half inch either way, it would have cleaved the entire cranium. Then the succeeding blows would certainly have been fatal. As it was, the blows merely glanced off his scalp. He nearly drowned, however, from both the sea and the booze."

"Can he speak?"

"I don't think he'll come around completely for another forty-eight or so hours. That's the usual time in such cases. He's probably very groggy or confused or in shock."

Ovens' eyes, however, seemed to contradict the assessment of the insouciant young doctor. Dark brown, almost black, they told McGarr that Ovens knew the score: that his was not merely a medical problem that a favorable prognosis could eliminate, that whoever had done this to him had a very good reason, and those eyes, suddenly seeming very old, realized his troubles weren't over.

"Can you hear me?" McGarr asked him.

Nothing, not even his eyes, moved.

McGarr began twirling the key on the float that they had found aboard the *Virelay.* "I know you can. You heard what the doctor said, I saw your eyes following the conversation. I'm Inspector McGarr and this is my wife, Noreen."

Still Ovens' eyes didn't even blink. "No need for you to acknowledge what I'm saying. We'll get around to that a little later. Let me tell you what we know. Horace Hubbard, the yacht-club steward, attacked you."

Ovens' eyes didn't move.

"Because he's in love with your girl, the one with the flat in Ballsbridge." McGarr was bending over him now, nearly whispering into his ear.

"Right after hitting you, the two of them disappeared. We've learned they plan to get married."

Noreen moved toward McGarr as though wanting to stop him.

Still nothing.

"He pulled the sea cock and *Virelay* sank."

Nothing again.

McGarr straightened up and asked the doctor, "Forty-eight hours?"

"Maybe more, maybe less. It may well be that he does not remember the incident and will not for whole years. Perhaps only psychoanalysis will allow the man to recover the details in all their particularity."

That still wasn't what McGarr believed. The young doctor sounded like a textbook. McGarr had gained his experience firsthand, and he had the feeling that this man had understood all and had chosen not to talk. If so, from the little that McGarr already knew about Ovens, he would be a tough, if not impossible, nut to crack.

"Is he under sedation?" Noreen asked.

"A morphine base for pain. I'm sure he has a massive headache."

McGarr took the young doctor's elbow and began walking him down the ward toward the stairwell. He was a tall, thick-set, and healthy-looking—pink complexion, bushy blond hair—Irishman who, McGarr speculated, in other times and without the advantages of his education, would have become a policeman. "You and I will probably find ourselves working together on many cases in the next twenty years. I'm a man with a good memory and I'm grateful. I'm wondering," said McGarr in a low voice, "could you move him to a private room?"

"Who would pay?" O'Higgins asked.

"Ah"—McGarr didn't have the vaguest idea who would pay and speculated Ovens or his wealthy female friend would eventually have to bear the expense—"we'll work something out. In spite of his appearance, he comes from a wealthy background"—which wasn't far from the truth. "Also, young man, I have a favor to ask." McGarr stopped him on the stairwell. "I'm going to tell the paper Ovens died."

O'Higgins looked down at McGarr with profound incredulity. "You can't do that."

"And why not?"

"Because it's a lie. It's just not true."

Noreen had walked to the window where, smiling, she looked out on the lawn and the stretch of dual carriageway that ran past the hospital.

"Not really, when you consider it'll help us catch the person who did this to Ovens, probably prevent the deranged person from doing this to others. Right? And don't worry. I'll take the full responsibility. It's the only way I know of popping the bugger who did this in the jug. You just make yourself unavailable for comment, if somebody should ask, which they won't. The death of a Yank from seemingly accidental causes isn't the sort of scoop any reporter used to the blood bath in the North would pursue. Are you the only doctor on the case now?"

"Yes—I cover postoperative and mild traumatic care. Only in severe cases do I consult the . . ." O'Higgins smiled slightly. ". . . older doctors." Younger Irish doctors were better trained than the older generations, and there was a certain amount of professional enmity between the groups. "I can't envision any complications with Ovens' recuperation. Even his liver may recover here."

"Will you do it?"

"I don't know. Are you *the* Peter McGarr, the one who worked for Criminal Justice in Paris?"

"Yes."

Noreen turned to hear the exchange.

"I was studying in Paris at the time. Do you remember the editorial in *Le Monde* that said the only reason you kept making all the big arrests was that, being Irish, you had a certain innate guile that allowed you to think like a criminal and keep one step ahead of them?"

McGarr began to laugh. He had a framed copy in his study on the second floor of his Rathmines home. The *Irish Press*, giving secondary coverage to the story, had been outraged and had begun an editorial cat fight with the big Parisian newspaper, which ended with the *Press*'s asking McGarr how he could continue working in a country whose largest newspaper had denigrated him so. The answer was simple: no criminal investigative agency had ever accepted any of his many applications for a senior position in Ireland, and the contention of *Le Monde* was largely true. McGarr had a definite penchant for intrigue.

O'Higgins continued. "I loved that piece. I showed it to all the guys and told them to watch out."

"Will you do it, then?"

"I don't know. This is so highly irregular. What if—"

"Don't you worry about a thing. I know how this place works. The old boys won't even know it happened. We'll tweak their noses."

McGarr and Noreen started down the stairs.

O'Higgins shouted after them, "And, Inspector, I'm training to be a pathologist here. Did I tell you that? In a couple of years we'll be working together for sure."

"That I should live so long," McGarr said to Noreen. McGarr had had to wait until somebody died for a position to be offered to him. He was forty-four at the time. O'Higgins would find the post of chief pathologist even more exclusive. McGarr mused that in ten years O'Higgins would probably be chief pathologist in Rochester, New York, or Brisbane, Australia, or some other place of exile.

Noreen and McGarr drove straight to Dublin Castle.

The soldier at the guard house was surprised to see McGarr. "The few who were here, Inspector, have just left," he said into the open window of the Cooper. "Only the night shift is left."

"We won't be long, Gerald." McGarr knew the guard had a sweetheart who would come by to keep him company once the department chiefs had left for the weekend.

Dublin Castle is the set of mean brick buildings from which the British directed the subjugation of Ireland. No more than a quadrangle of barracks houses set on a small rise, its treeless courtyard was the site of innumerable political assassinations. It was McGarr's opinion that the Irish Free State had made a big mistake installing even some of their own police and military here. They should have dynamited, then leveled the spot as a symbolic gesture, or failing that, opened it as a memorial to those who had died in the six-hundred-year battle for freedom.

With the lights off and the day dwindling, the corridors leading to the wing McGarr's staff occupied were as dark as he had ever seen them. The few rays of slanting late-afternoon sunlight could not penetrate the rain-streaked and dusty windows. A dim glow alone outlined the battered furniture and heaving floors. The place still smelled like a barracks: old leather, dubbin, tons of aging paper in file cabinets, floor wax, and the pine-scented cleanser the British had used in the cells, all too familiar to McGarr whose official responsibilities had made the Castle the part of his life he enjoyed least. The one portrait he allowed in his office was that of Wolfe Tone.

While Noreen sat in his chair and, swiveling it away from the desk, looked out the west window at the startling contrast of the greenery in Phoenix Park, a mile distant, McGarr scrawled several notes and then copied them into their running log book. In a country where pubs were social centers and the imagination was as yet unshackled, McGarr believed the procedure entirely appropriate. More than one of his men had a touch of Ireland's special failings.

First he ordered Ward to pick up Brud Clare and grill him until he revealed the woman's name, to learn everything he could about Horace C. K. Hubbard right down to dental charts. He then sent Kevin Slattery to lawyer Greaney's office on Leeson Street to find out who owned 17 Percy Place, who leased flat 5A, and who paid the rent. Paul Sinclair, a new man who had returned home after seventeen years on the Sydney police force, was to stake out the apartment. McGarr assigned Bernie McKeon and Harry Greaves the thankless task of canvassing the entire hill behind the Killiney Yacht Club. There remained the possibility that another shut-in like Moran might have been scanning the docks when Ovens was attacked. Also, a tourist or sightseer might have snapped a picture at that moment. He asked them to assign a few uniformed men to cover all the chemist and photography shops, even the Agfa-Gevaert and Kodak processing plants, to see if anybody might remember handling a tourist's or sightseer's photos of Killiney Bay on a sunny afternoon. Friday afternoon, the weather had been spectacular.

Midway through this procedure, Noreen asked, "Shall I get hold of Liam O'Shaughnessy and ask him if he could arrange to rent his brother's lobster boat for tomorrow? How long does it take to run out to Inishmore? I've never been to Kilronan."

McGarr nodded, then added to McKeon's orders the job of examining the Loretto Avenue garage in Dun Laoghaire that Ovens had used as a workshop. He called the home of a reporter friend and told him about his plan to release news of Ovens' death. The man concurred and thought he could slip a back-page article and an obituary short into the Sunday papers.

Noreen had taken McGarr's phone directory from the top drawer of his desk. Both knew their first order of business was to find out if the attack on Ovens had resulted from something to do with the gun oil on the cabin flooring of *Virelay.* If so, the case would then become enormously complicated, and McGarr would have to use his contacts in the contending factions of the IRA to learn more. Because of the treacherous waters of Galway Bay, especially near Inishmore, an island some twenty miles out to sea, it was difficult for authorities to patrol the area. A boat with a skilled pilot or experienced captain, such as Ovens, well might have negotiated the channel and off-loaded a cargo. Spud Murphy, the Inishmore IRA contact, owed McGarr at least that much information for a favor done him in the past. Also, McGarr was tolerated by many elements of the IRA. He seldom had trouble learning the details of past operations.

Noreen said the phone rang only once before O'Shaughnessy picked it up, announcing "Bronx Zoo" into the mouthpiece. With the noise of a Gaelic band in the background, the huge man pretended he couldn't hear her. He was half lit and had every intention of torching whatever remained, he told her. A party was in progress, just the sort of house gathering McGarr enjoyed most, with poteen and roast pork and, outside, miles of rock walls, small cottages with yellow lights in the windows, and the cleanest air in all of Europe to clear one's head. They were only 110 miles away. The Cooper made it in less than two hours. McGarr found that in no way was he dressed out of character here. The sweater was right, and the rest of their garb was accepted as perfectly appropriate because they, friends of a friend, chose to wear short pants and canvas boating shoes. Killiney Bay, Dun Laoghaire, and Dublin itself were still part of that other culture's pale.

3

From offshore, Inishmore was a block of shale. Gorse was shaggy on top, bright green dappled pink and windswept. Sea gulls in legion flew out to meet the lobster boat as it bucked the Atlantic swells.

This coast, McGarr mused, thinking of his years in France, was indeed a *côte sauvage,* the ragged end of the continental land mass. Gulf Stream tides and ocean storms pounded away at the rocky beaches and precipitous cliffs. The wind was roaring, impelling the steady rain in horizontal torrents that stung the face. The hull clapped, shuddered, then sank on every second wave.

Not a house was in sight through the driving mist until the cliffs rose into a massive promontory. Around this Liam's brother, Michael, spun the wheel. Once past, the land softened dramatically, although the rocky coast was still hazardous. A cluster of limed cottages with thatched roofs and nets drying on driftwood racks appeared through the mist. The old boat needed all the power its diesel could muster to keep from broaching on a wide shoal over which the surf boiled. Michael headed up into the wind, and McGarr, being dashed with spray and pelted with wind, ran the boat hook through the eye of a permanent mooring. He pulled the barnacle-encrusted line onto the foredeck and secured it to the cleat.

A double-ended beach boat came out to lighter them ashore. Liam had reached Spud Murphy on the wireless. The long boat with eight men manning the oars pitched and yawed and finally, mounting the crest of a wave, surfed ashore.

The beach of pulverized oyster shells made one color with the seafoam, driving mist, ashen skies, and cottages in Kilronan: a grey as glossy as from a tube of oil paint. Upon this background, the beach boat, the tanned faces and wet woolen clothes of the crew, oars over their shoulders, seemed to be imposed starkly in too sharp a focus. Thus the men looked older than they were, the boat battered, the cottages mere shelters from these unremitting elements.

McGarr was drawn to this place with what he well knew was the appreciation of a dilettante. This was the Ireland of the picture books he had read as a child. Here life was hard. The sea yielded her bounty at a price exacted in toil and life loss. Nearly a third of the men ever born on this island had been lost at sea. The road, like the beaches, was a glistening surface of crushed shells.

Murphy met them in a small building that abutted the seawall on the outskirts of Kilronan. A plank between two porter barrels sufficed as a bar. Coal oil, dried fish, candy, tobacco, oilskins, rubber boots, and week-old newspapers were also offered.

Murphy was a stout man even shorter then McGarr. The name Spud suited him with great precision, for his face was a fleshy welter of moles and bumps, his skin deep brown. His eyes were dark. He wore a soft cap, black rubber bib overalls that formed boots at the feet, and a filthy tweed sportscoat. In spite of the pipe he drew on so often that he seemed forever wrapped in a cloud of acrid blue smoke, Murphy stank like a mackerel. It had been this sour stench that had landed him in McGarr's Dublin Castle office two years before.

A customs officer at the Dun Laoghaire docks had asked Murphy if he had anything to declare. "Only a couple of fowling pieces for grousing, don't you know," the old fisherman had declared. It had been the middle of the winter and a storm had sickened many of the mailboat passengers in the line behind Murphy. The officer was about to let him pass, since the top piece was indeed a shotgun and the stocks of the others, all of which had been stripped to components, seemed similar, when he detected the reek of the mackinaw Murphy was wearing. The officer then consulted the address on Murphy's identity papers. The only grousing Inishmore offered was that which Murphy could do with his mouth. All of the guns but one had been M14s. McGarr, wanting to cull the favors of as many IRA contacts as possible, and knowing his countrymen to be inveterate gossips, told the prosecuting magistrate that since none of the guns had been loaded, no crime had been committed. Murphy had left Dublin Castle with his shotgun in hand and a good word for McGarr.

"Chief Inspector," Murphy said in a voice so high it was like the warble of a bird, "have y' been exiled? You can't be planning to fish since there's not a mullet between here and the Grand Banks this past week. Good to see you." He extended his hand. "I recognize this whale to yer right"—he meant O'Shaughnessy, who was paying the proprietress for the jug of poteen he had lifted onto the plank—"and his squid of a brother Michael. How are you, boys?" Murphy shook with them. "And who, dear God, might this be?" A small coal sputtered from his pipe and fell to the floor. He made as though he would put his arm around Noreen's shoulder, saying, "A trim red woman with lots of fire. Sure and I'd give you a hug myself if I hadn't come from roiling in the 'flits' of several species of bait fish we peddle in Dublin." Like many men who lead solitary lives, the mere sight of a visitor made Murphy jolly. "People there, they tell me, are nothing but carp themselves, swimming in that turbid bowl the Liffey forms between Rathfarnum and Swords."

Said McGarr, "Speaking of fish, Spud, have you shot any with automatic weapons recently? Meet my wife, Noreen." And then to her, he added, "He'll grouse as much now as when I had him on the hot seat at the Castle."

"Pleased, pleased." Murphy's eyes fixed on Noreen's, then darted to her chin, her nose, her tight copper curls, and elsewhere.

Since Murphy's entrance the proprietress, an old woman with a red face and pure white hair that stuck from her head in patches, had been gesturing to him with her eyes. She wished to speak to Murphy behind the curtain in back of the candy counter. Finally, she said, "Murph, boy, may I see you for a second out back?" and she stepped behind the blind.

"It's just my girl, Eileen. Jealous, I should think." He stuck only his head beyond the curtain and whispers passed between them. The wind howled through the chinks in the roof corrugations and eddied the thick clouds from Murphy's pipe.

Their consultation gradually rose in volume so that McGarr heard the words ". . . police . . . jail . . . bloody Tanner . . ." from Eileen. Then Murphy, pulling her by the wrist into the room, said, "This is Eileen McFadden, my fiancée. Chief of Detectives McGarr and his lovely wife, Noreen. I take it you know that walrus and his brother the giant grouper from Dublin."

"Shall we flatten him?" Liam asked his brother.

"Not without some hot oil and a pan."

Plainly embarrassed, Eileen tried to smooth the tufts of her hair. She then wiped her hands on the apron several times.

"Pour yourself a sup, girl," said Murphy, "just in case they've come for you."

Reaching for Eileen's hand, which was as rough as nailboard, McGarr said, "It's not Eileen I'm after but some information about the schooner *Virelay.* It put in here about a year and a half ago."

Eileen flushed. She turned her head sharply to Murphy and said, "Oh, God, didn't I know it. Didn't I say it'd come to this. Don't tell him, Spud. Don't do it." She pronounced his nickname "Shpood."

McGarr added, "Ovens was attacked Friday. Head split open."

"Muscha—say no more, no more," the old woman muttered as though to herself. She poured a drink into a custard cup the like of which the others were using and tossed it back. She wiped her mouth with her apron.

"I'm investigating only the attack."

"Where did it happen?" Murphy asked, reaching for his cup.

"Killiney Bay."

"Then why come here?"

"I think you know. We found gun oil on the cabin flooring of the boat. His charts show us he was headed here. I'm not interested in the whereabouts of whatever arms the boat might have carried, who handled them, or where they were stored, only in the person or persons who tried to kill Ovens. I've come here because we've been unable to learn much about the man. He stumps me. One of our few clues is the gun oil on the floor. Was Inishmore *Virelay*'s landfall?"

"Not a word, not a word," muttered Eileen.

Murphy flicked a thumbnail up the head of a match, which burst into flame.

"Ah, Spud boy, don't. Don't. He'll clap you in the can as quick as you can say King Billy was a bloody bastard."

When all turned to her, she said defiantly, "Well, he was! Does that upset you? If it does, you've come to the wrong place."

Murphy sighed, the smoke pouring through his nostrils. He took the pipe from his mouth. "I knew this would happen to them."

"Them?" McGarr asked.

"Please, God, don't let the foolish man say more."

"Ovens and his sweetheart. A fetching thing, she was. Ample." He nudged Noreen's elbow and chuckled.

Noreen said, "I thought you liked trim women with lots of fire."

"I like women, woman. Give us a squeeze. I can tell you're a girl with a good ear for a deserved compliment." Murphy pulled Noreen to him and kissed her cheek.

"Listen to him, would you? And why do you think we've been unmarried all these years? It's barbarous the way he'll chase a skirt. The merest flutter of a hem in the wind!"

But then Murphy's mood sobered. "Sure, there *was* something tragic about the two of them."

"What was her name?"

"Lee was what he called her. It's the American for Lea, she told me."

"Irish?"

"I think so, but, you know, a city girl."

"Last name?"

"I never caught it, but later I was told by a certain well-placed Dublin fellow I should feel lucky I didn't. Somebody very, very important she's connected with, you see."

"In what way?"

"Don't know."

"And do you have a hint who that might be?"

"No. I figured it was better not to know, in case—and then here you've appeared and fortunately I'm unable to tell you more."

"Good boy, Spud. Good lad." Eileen reached for the jug.

"Tragic in what way was their relationship?" asked Noreen.

"Love stories are dear to the hearts of all beautiful women." Murphy took the opportunity to give Noreen another squeeze. "Sure, and I could tell you a barrel of them garnered from personal experience."

"Take my advice, y' talk too much. And keep your bloody mashers to yourself. In that barrel of which he speaks," Eileen confided to Noreen, "he plays the part of the worm, if you can understand me completely." She tossed back her drink.

Now the wind was howling through the chinks in the roof.

"Ovens arrived here a confused man. He had not known what the cargo she had asked him to transport really was. Small arms—sure, he had agreed to carry that much. But—"

Eileen moaned.

"—jelly, rocket launchers, and the sort of antipersonnel mines the Geneva Convention should ban? He found them hidden under the guns when he tried to repair his busted motor.

"And the girl got here the next day saying she knew nothing about it." Murphy drew on the whiskey and looked out the side window where the sea was clapping into the wall and sending up spumes of spray that blew across the road. "Just two kids the Provos played for fools." Murphy mused for a second. "Or were they? I wondered, to tell you the truth, if she wasn't acting. Something about her was just not right. He landed. I radioed my contact. She got here within hours, as though she had been waiting in Galway City. He told her about his finding the other weapons. She seemed to share his dismay—"

Eileen finished the story. "And three hours later, a boatload of gunmen arrived, stuck up half the town, and took everything off that boat including galley knives. When the Yank objected, two others held the man like so"—Eileen threw back her arms as though being held; suddenly she was very drunk—"and the chief bully boy beat him senseless." She tossed her head from side to side. "And the little skirt as much as says, 'Ah, what the hell. That's the way it goes,' like those brigands had stole a tub of tripes. She then pays me brother Mick a small fortune to haul her to Limerick, of all places. As far as I'm concerned, that's where she belongs."

"Like she knew—" Murphy tried to say.

"Like she knew what was up all along. There you have it, the unvarnished truth."

"Are they married?" Noreen asked.

Again Eileen answered. "Perhaps, but not to each other. She had a ring mark on her fourth finger left hand that was bigger than the ring she wore. There's certain of us what notices them things." Without turning her head from McGarr, she directed her eyeballs, which now were as red as her face, to Murphy.

"Now that was a detail I missed completely," Murphy said sheepishly into his raised custard cup. He drank, then explained. "You see, Eily and me are getting married just as soon as my aged mother passes on. We're waiting so we can have a home to call our own. Building materials is scarce in these parts, and what with the inflation and all—"

"And she's a relic, that bitch!" Eileen hollered. "I promise, I'll do the hag in one of these days!" Murphy led her behind the curtain.

As Noreen and McGarr stepped outside, they heard her say, "You're a divil with the ladies, Murph boy. Give us a touch. Who knows—it'll probably be all we'll have to remember."

"Later, later," Murphy said and returned to the O'Shaughnessy brothers to help dent the crock.

The McGarrs walked arm and arm down the road directly into the blast off the water. The whiskey had made them warm enough to ignore the cold wind that thundered in their ears, tight enough to marvel at the cascading water. They tried to talk without success. This place was harsh, but so different from mild Dublin they loved it. Behind a low stone outcropping, a myriad of bright wild flowers thrived in patches of yellow and deep red.

They had to spend the night in Eileen's guest room, since the seas had risen too high for them to return to Galway. The room was on the second floor, its bed a deep valley that threw them together. Toward dawn, the weather broke and the sun rose so bright it woke them. Eileen was already up with hot tea, fried herring, scones, and marmalade. Over breakfast Spud Murphy tried to convince McGarr that he should join the IRA. It was his patriotic duty to the ideal of a thirty-two-county Republic such as what the martyrs, "the poets and dreamers of the Easter Rising had envisioned." McGarr told him he was neither a poet nor a dreamer, and the thought of becoming a martyr he found positively chilling. With that, Eileen broke out a small crock and they shared several libations.

At the dock in Galway City, a Garda sergeant was waiting for McGarr with the message to call the Pierce Hotel in Naas and ask for the minister for justice. McGarr imagined Horace C. K. Hubbard had contacted his own well-placed friends.

McGarr was wrong.

From the moment he saw the minister standing at the hotel bar, he knew the request for this meeting was in some way extraordinary. A tall man whose paunch had fallen, David Horrigan grasped a whiskey in his right hand and stared into it as though trying to divine some mystery at the bottom of the glass. The minister, however, did not drink. And although the bar with its flagstone floor and shaded windows was cool, Horrigan's brow was beaded with sweat. Because of the recent change in government ministers, McGarr didn't know the man well and wondered why he was away from his office on a working day and why he had asked McGarr to meet him here, outside Dublin.

Plainly, Horrigan hadn't expected Noreen to be along and her presence irked him. His pleasantries seemed forced. At length, he asked her if he might have a word with McGarr alone, and leaving her to lunch in the dining room with the publican's wife, whom Noreen knew from her days at University College, Dublin, the minister for justice and McGarr climbed a flight of stairs to his suite on the second floor, which Horrigan explained so: "Like you, Peter, I grew up in Dublin on Clanbrassil Street near the Four Courts. Like yours, my family was poor. I've been going through your dossier, which I took the liberty of lifting from the files a few moments after you left the Castle Saturday afternoon."

"Gerald told me everybody had left." Horrigan's office was not in Dublin Castle but on St. Stephen's Green, and whereas the minister was responsible for the Garda, as a politician he did not normally have free access to their files.

"I was hoping it would seem that way." Horrigan was nervous, and his hand shook as he fit the door key into its lock. "Where was I?"

"Hotel living." McGarr was now on his toes in every sense. Seldom had he ever allowed a governmental officer of Horrigan's rank to engage him in such familiar conversation. Much political in-fighting was transpiring in Dublin mostly because of the differing approaches to the trouble in the North. Horrigan had made no bones about his position: a united Ireland controlled in Dublin. He wanted England to purchase at market price the land and real property of any Scotch-Irishman who couldn't live with a Dublin-based government, and then have England set up a program of resettlement back where Cromwell's campaigners had come from, across the Irish Sea in Scotland and northern England. He wanted the Dublin government to repudiate the 1937 constitution that had declared a special relationship between the Roman Catholic Church and Ireland and had prohibited divorce and contraception. McGarr thought this an interesting but naïve plan, impracticable and designed only to put Horrigan in office. It had proved tremendously popular.

Horrigan swung the door wide and McGarr stepped into a room appointed not in standard hotel gauche but rather a period setting that McGarr judged as accurate and tasteful as any of the mansions he had visited during his many burglary investigations. Most of the pieces were Chippendale originals. A finely detailed oriental rug with blue and green patterning on a beige background covered most of a parquet floor. The windows were French, specially constructed in the recent past. Brilliant linen drapes gathered the light from the courtyard. "My father was a farrier who worked for the Shelbourne Hotel whenever they had too much work for their own man to handle. I, being the oldest, was let out as a step-and-fetch-it, bootblack, you know what I mean." Horrigan had opened a sideboard that contained a number of crystal decanters below. "And I said to myself that if some day I could afford it, neither house nor farm nor boat nor castle would be my abode. Nothing but a hotel for me with hot-and-cold running servants, a kitchen, bar, stables, and lots of company. And so here I am. Malt?"

"Please."

Horrigan poured McGarr a generous drink and dropped the stopper back into the neck of the decanter.

McGarr was trying to remember the details of this man's life. His address in Dublin *was* the Shelbourne, in fact a suite of rooms on the top floor overlooking St. Stephen's Green. He had made his money by slippery practices. As the government's lawyer, he had negotiated with a cartel of international oil companies the establishment of a deep-water port in Bantry Bay that could accommodate the supertankers of the future. When the combine came to purchase land for their storage tanks and refinery, David Horrigan's father, mother, sisters, and brothers just happened to be the new owners of every square foot of waterfront property along the projected site. Horrigan had resigned his post and had remained unavailable for comment for nearly ten years, long enough time, he must have felt, for his gains to have become legitimized. He surfaced as a major contributor to the coffers of the Fianna Fail resurgence.

To the carping queries of a journalist during a television interview, Horrigan, a man with a lively intelligence, had explained his checkered career so: "And how did those other politicians, the ones with the English names we still kowtow to and let control disproportionate shares of the countryside, gather their fortunes? They made laws that declared them more equal, allowed them to steal us blind, and when there was nothing left they clapped us into a slavery more vicious and pervasive than that of Czarist Russia. Why? Because we were 'barbarous,' which meant we no longer owned anything. When I was growing up, their cry was no different. The LAW!, they shouted whenever any of us started agitating for a redistribution of the country's resources. I decided I would study this law which had been so good to so few. What did I learn? That the law was the tool by which the name Horrigan could appear on the deeds of several thousand acres of Bantry Bay shoreland instead of the name Guinness or Ormond or Watson. I don't like the way things are any more than other patriotic Irishmen, but, since they are, then I must conform until I enjoy a position preeminent enough to allow me and my people—the ones from the Dublin gutters like me, the ones from the rustic poverty of the country like my wife's people—to effect sweeping change in this country. It is to this end I am working." That statement and his stand on the Northern Ireland question gave him a seat in the Dail. His contributions to the party gave him his cabinet post.

Handing McGarr the drink, Horrigan scrutinized the detective in a way that made McGarr self-conscious. He was still in his boating garb. "You don't know me," Horrigan said, pacing in front of the mantel, on which the gold balls of an eight-day clock spun silent in a vacuum, "nor I you, outside of the bare details of our lives. It's because of our backgrounds—Dublin, poverty, the law—that I chose to call you and not somebody from Internal Security or some other agency. What I'm going to put to you, you needn't accept, since my request cannot be official." Horrigan turned to McGarr suddenly. "In this I'm thinking of you. If I have to go, no reason I should take anybody with me, much less you, who haven't an idea of what's happened." Greying hair curled onto his brow. His face was characteristically Irish: bulbous nose, puffy cheeks and jowls. He was not a handsome man. His dark blue pin-striped suit was expensive, but he appeared uncomfortable in it.

He turned toward the window. "Sometimes I wonder how things happen and why so fast. It seems only weeks ago that I left school, got married, felt so young and enthusiastic. Now"—he let his narrow shoulders fall—"I feel so old."

"How old are you?" asked McGarr, somewhat embarrassed at this confessional monologue.

"Forty-three."

He looked at least fifty.

"I thought I saw things a little clearer than other people, you know, what was happening here in Ireland, what I should do to get ahead, how I could help myself and the country, the sort of family I wanted, the friends, the whole . . . works." He let out a little laugh. "You know, I was wrong. It made me happy thinking I knew, and in that way I deluded myself no less than the dreamer who crawls into the amber world of a porter bottle." He moved to the sideboard and poured himself a whiskey.

"Certainly that won't help," said McGarr. "Tell me why you've called me here."

"I've watched you work. You're from Swift's Dublin. That's the sensibility I work in, but being a public man, I keep my kit bag of verbal palliatives close by."

McGarr shook his head. "I'm from McGarr's Dublin."

"That's what I mean, *just* what I mean!" Horrigan sat opposite McGarr in a wing-back chair that wrapped him in shadow. He took a sip of whiskey and shuddered as he swallowed. "We deal in the real, no—"

"Bull shit," said McGarr.

"Exactly. Now, this is what has happened, why I called you here. Did you work on the Bombing Report?"

McGarr nodded. He had headed the investigation, and he knew Horrigan knew that.

"Then you know it blames the IRA, says it was a cheap political ploy. They had hoped to blame it on some one of the 'loyal orders' or some Protestant extremist group and thereby bring the fighting home to the Republic. They hoped to arouse public sentiment and support. Do you know my position?"

"On the IRA?"

Horrigan nodded.

"Not in so many words." The IRA was as complex an organization as could be devised by the Irish people, who are an enigma unto themselves, since, unlike the government, it claimed to represent their dreams as well as the most glorious moments of their past.

Horrigan said, "I support them."

"All of them?" Some IRA elements were committed to urban terrorism.

"*All* of them. The rhetoric means nothing to me, nor the violence. For every drop of British blood now being shed up there, they have sucked buckets of ours. People say, why those British colonists have been living in Ulster for three hundred years! That just goes to show how tight is the iron grip those patriots, who now call themselves Provos or Maoists or whatever, are trying to break. In 1916 the average Dubliner thought the show at the GPO was a bloody farce."

McGarr nodded and sipped from his whiskey.

"In any case, my copy of the report is missing."

McGarr looked up. To his knowledge, the report was still most secret and political dynamite of the worst sort, since it blamed the IRA for the blast. And for the government it was a no-win situation: they had seemed to sit idly by while this organization, or some part of it, bombed downtown Dublin during rush hour.

Horrigan continued, "It was a question of degrees—how much of the report we were going to release, how much innuendo we might have been able to create."

McGarr furrowed his brow. He didn't care for politics or politicians one bit. He had seen too many competent policemen become patsies for wily politicians.

"You know, we could go to the IRA and say, look, we know some part of your outfit did it, but there's no reason to bring down the government too. We've been good to you. The arrests we've made, as you well know, have been *pro forma.* Here are your options or we'll round up and intern every single IRA suspect we can find and then release the whole report: one, give us the names of the bunch of bastards who did it along with the evidence to hang them; two, give us some evidence to blame it on a British provocateur or any other organization but the IRA and its affiliates. Of course, we'll hope they don't just laugh at us. Mass arrests and internment would bring this government down in days. The people wouldn't stand for it."

McGarr felt very uncomfortable and needed another whiskey badly. Politics blurred things so. He had been one of the first to arrive in Nassau Street after the blast. He had found a little girl with a leg and a hand blown off. That was wrong, no two ways about it. He wanted to get back to the facts. "Was there another copy?"

"Not in this form. I was going to go over it Thursday night one final time before we retyped it and sent it to the Taoseaich. This was the unedited version."

"Where was it?"

"In the sideboard under lock and key, of course."

McGarr could have gotten into that sideboard with a toothpick. His glance was more toward the whiskey decanter than the door lock. A person who didn't drink had no idea of the timing necessary to be a successful host. McGarr imagined one whiskey might last Horrigan an eternity.

"You see, this is most embarrassing to me. In order to get elected I had to support the violence in the North. Now, when it happens here in my own electorate and I'm in charge of the investigation and it seems like the IRA might get blamed, I suddenly dispose of the report. Or, just as bad, I release only a part of the report and the whole thing then turns up in the press."

"So somebody wants to get you and not necessarily the government."

"That's why I called you. It seems to be some sort of private vendetta. I believe firmly that if I were to resign today, the report would either be returned or the parts that this government would doubtless eliminate or obscure will never surface." McGarr said noth ing, only looked at the minister, who added, "But I don't want to resign voluntarily. I've waited a dozen years to get here. And where I'm headed I've wanted all of my life."

"No forced entry. You must suspect somebody and not just the"—he waved his hand—"IRA. Who else knew you had the report with you?"

"My secretary, my first assistant, and"—Horrigan raised his glass to his mouth; he said over the surface of the liquor—"my wife." He wet his upper lip. "My secretary is a widow near retirement who lives in Dublin. Both of her brothers died in the Troubles, both with the IRA."

"Name?"

"Neila Monahan, two eighty-three North Circular Road."

"Your first assistant?"

"A literary man. Sometimes submits poems in Irish to the *Times.*" Horrigan watched McGarr finish the whiskey in his tumbler. "Aren't you going to take any of this down?"

"No." McGarr never took notes, he simply concentrated all his intelligence on the vital details of every case. He could summon from memory the names, addresses, and distinguishing characteristics of all persons he had arrested and many of the others who had figured in his investigations.

"His name is Carleton Driver and he lives on Fitzwilliam Square."

"Age?"

"Mid-forties."

"Married?"

"To literature and the great Celtic oral tradition, if you know what I mean."

"How is his office work?"

"Phenomenal, when he's there. If I only had half his brains and he half my sense!"

"Political leanings?"

"Definitely left."

"Temperamental?"

"Yes."

"Where does he drink?"

"McDaid's."

"Why do you think your wife stole the report?"

This took Horrigan by surprise.

"Would you mind if—" McGarr began to stand. He wanted another drink, even if he had to extort it. He had the feeling that much more information than what the minister had offered was yet to come.

"Oh, please do. Excuse me."

McGarr poured himself a very sufficient drink.

"Have you people been conducting your own investigation?"

"No."

"Then how—?"

"Call it a leap of faith." McGarr offered him a Woodbine.

Horrigan accepted, saying, "I haven't had one of these for years."

"Don't make it a habit. They tell me they're a force more lethal than the IRA. You don't live together?" In spite of the care taken with the details of the room, there was not one feminine touch anywhere. Everything was too ordered, nothing placed by whimsy.

Horrigan looked askance at McGarr. "Has another minister asked you to—"

McGarr shook his head. "You obviously credit me with knowing my profession, otherwise you wouldn't have asked me here."

Horrigan stood and walked to the window as if he wished to heighten the confessional nature of the exchange. He drew on the cigarette and blew out the smoke immediately. "What can I tell you about Leona?"

McGarr, perhaps because of the Ovens case, had not quite understood the minister's pronunciation of the name. "Excuse me, what is her name?"

Horrigan turned to him. "Leona. Do you know her?"

McGarr shook his head.

The minister turned back to the view of the courtyard. It had begun to rain and the sky was slate. "When we first married, we were poor but plucky. Both fresh out of university—she teaching national school here in Dublin for money that wouldn't keep a friar in holy water, me trying to scrounge up legal work. I prosecuted my first case against the Dublin County Council when my maiden aunt slipped on a puddle of ice in front of her flat and broke her hip."

"Children?"

"Three and grown. The youngest is a senior sophister at Trinity, of all places."

"When did you begin living apart?"

Horrigan turned his head sharply to him. He honestly couldn't remember. He walked to the table, picked up his glass, and then went to the sideboard. "Maybe fifteen years ago. The youngest was walking, I remember, and just about to enter kindergarten. We never talked about her leaving me, mind you, or about separation, living apart, or divorce. I had begun to make big money a few years before that, and we started adding a place here, a suite of rooms in London. We bought a boat."

"What kind?"

"All kinds. She traded boats, bought, sold, rented, leased them in such multiplicity I don't know what we own right now myself."

"You don't sail yourself?" McGarr was now fitting the pieces of what the minister was telling him into the Ovens case. He wondered why the man had really called him here like this. Could it be that *he* had attacked Ovens and, definitely a nervous type, couldn't wait for the investigation to uncover his wife's involvement with the man?

Horrigan chuckled into the whiskey glass. "I would have liked to sail and now realize that for the sake of my marriage I should have, but I either told myself I didn't have the time or really didn't have it. Another thing is the training. I tried it once, but I was born a Dublin guttersnipe. Do you know the sort of person who sails in Ireland, Peter?"

"I know the sort of person who sails." McGarr thought briefly of Ovens, who was an American, and then Horace C. K. Hubbard. McGarr had tried unsuccessfully to know some of the people who had sailed on the Riviera. To him they were different—ignorantly exclusive, inveterately romantic, eccentric.

"They're born to it. In her own way, my wife was too. Her father used to build boats for them at Cobh, and because of that they accepted her in a patronizing way, if you know what I mean. *Later*"—Horrigan raised his voice—"they accepted her because she could buy and sell the lot of them with the small change in her checkbook!" Merely talking about this situation seemed to anger Horrigan, but McGarr wished he knew the man better. There seemed to be just the slightest bit of affectation in his speech, a small touch of the histrionic in his gestures.

McGarr sipped from his whiskey.

Now Horrigan was leaning against the sideboard. "And so ours became one of the first of what they now call an 'open' marriage. She did her thing, as the saying goes, and I mine. Hers included several downright rotters. I hired Hugh Madigan—do you know him?"

McGarr nodded. Madigan was a private detective with offices in London.

"He told me that much. Along the way, about the time our oldest son became a research student in London, it became fashionable for certain 'Anglo-Irish' intellectuals—and I use both terms advisedly, Inspector McGarr—to champion the causes of the Bernadette Devlins of the North. Leona had money, you see, and Eoin—that's our son—was just at the age when a party with free booze would invariably draw a bunch of freeloading blowhards he thought brilliant. So Leona gave parties." Horrigan stubbed the cigarette butt into the ashtray. "She never seemed able to discriminate about people who weren't exactly Irish, exactly her age, and exactly from her station in life."

"But about you?"

"Yes, goddammit! About me she could give you a litany of my personal failings that would run to volumes, but about that collection of fairies and sycophants, moochers, drunks, and plain old con men she couldn't learn a thing. She became embroiled in some organization that had its base in the Bogside and its financial support in London. From the money she spent, I would believe she alone was its backer."

"How much?"

"Forty-seven thousand pounds! You could buy a bloody tank for that much! I often wonder how much of it was pissed over bars on its way from Euston Station to Belfast."

"Much of it, no doubt," McGarr said. He was acquainted with the habits of professional quasi-revolutionaries. It was a bunko game much practiced by a certain type of Irishman in London.

Horrigan poured himself another drink. "You know, she was always swinging between feeling guilty for having so much money to feeling inadequate that she hadn't had the money for very long at all. I told her that if the money bothered her so much I'd put some in a blind bank trust and she could go back to Cork and live the simple life."

"And?"

"Oh, Christ! It's gotten so I can't open my mouth in her presence. She called me a cheap bastard who with ill-gotten millions would deny her and her children the necessities of life."

McGarr stood, walked to the sideboard, poured himself another drink, and raising the glass to his mouth, looked directly into Horrigan's eyes. He asked, "Did *you* try to murder Bobby Ovens? Is that why you called me here? I'll find your fingerprints on that winch handle, blood spatters on your clothes, you know."

Again Horrigan was surprised that McGarr had jumped ahead of him. He looked away, out the French windows, into the courtyard below. "No, I didn't. Of all her . . . 'flings,' I think I liked him the best. At least he was genuine and not interested in her money."

"I understand she's a beautiful woman."

"Yes, she is that. Perhaps too beautiful."

"Younger than you?"

Horrigan was now becoming drunk. His eyes were filling. "Not in years."

"Do you think she tried to murder Ovens?"

Horrigan tried to take a big sip from the tumbler. The fluid splashed on his upper lip. He coughed. Taking a handkerchief from his pocket, he explained, "I got a telephone call from her Friday night. She wanted to know what I could do to hush up the whole thing. She told me she didn't do it but said the whole situation would prove terribly embarrassing for all of us, me included, should all the facts be known. I told her I couldn't do a thing. She berated me, as usual, for being spineless and, you know, 'bourgeois.' "

"Where is she now?"

"I don't know. I had the call traced and the operator told me it came from a coin box in Dublin."

"Do you know about the flat in Ballsbridge?"

"I do now."

"You mean since you checked the running log in my office. That's what you were doing in the Castle, wasn't it?"

Sheepishly, Horrigan nodded his head.

"Then your telling me that somebody stole the report was phony."

"No. Somebody stole it."

"But *not* the IRA. What reason would they have for wanting to ruin you? When you come right down to it, you're their best friend in the present government. Already some of the investigating officers have leaked enough information to the press to implicate them. When the report comes out, they'll just say some fanatic did it."

Horrigan shook his head. "No, *not* the IRA, at least from what I can learn from the sources I have in the official wing."

"May I use your phone?"

"Certainly."

McGarr finished his drink and dialed his office. "Bernie, please." When McKeon came on, he said, "I want you to pick up Carleton Driver at the Department of Justice and get a statement about his activities Thursday, Friday, and Saturday nights. Then put a tail on him."

"What's it about, chief?"

"It's better that you don't know."

"Hush-hush?" McKeon was from a small village in

Leitrim and had a love of intrigue, especially in high places.

"Also, put a tail on Neila Monahan, who works in the same office. I want discreet questions asked her neighbors about her activities Thursday, Friday, and Saturday nights. Lastly, when Liam O'Shaughnessy arrives, I want him to go to the Department of Justice in his plain clothes and take a statement from the minister for justice himself." Cupping the receiver with his hand, he asked Horrigan, "When will you be there?"

"I'd prefer him to come here."

"I wouldn't, if you don't mind."

"Two o'clock."

"At two." McGarr listened for a moment. McKeon thought he heard O'Shaughnessy coming down the hall. The huge man was a favorite in the Castle, his step and greeting unmistakable. When he got to the phone, McGarr said to him, "Bernie will tell you what I want, Liam. The statement you take from the minister will give you an idea of how important the situation is. I want you to put all your other work aside and concentrate on this investigation alone."

O'Shaughnessy began to complain. He had details to gather, reports to write.

"Put it all on my desk. I'll get Delaney to handle the paper and Boyle the leg work. Now—listen to me: *you* are in charge of this investigation entirely. I don't want to hear from you again until you've got things sorted out. Let me speak to Bernie."

Horrigan was agitated.

McGarr explained. "I'm not passing the buck. When the investigation begins to take shape, I'll take over. What I'm doing is institutionalizing the search, so that if the public prosecutor, the press, your political party, anybody wants to know what you or I or the department did once you found the papers missing, we can show them the record or present them with a battery of witnesses to prove this was no clandestine operation." McGarr resituated the phone. "Bernie? Who's waiting for me?"

"Just about everybody. What's all this about a 'clandestine operation,' boss? What's O'Shaughnessy got that I don't have? Mary and me were talking this over last night. Why is it you never give me the interesting assignments and always have me covering for you around here or shagging bird watchers out on Killiney Bay or tracking down shutterbugs in photography stores or speaking to a passel of Krauts in the Agfa-Gavaert factory, and just generally—"

"Bernie," McGarr cut in, "it's because you're a good detail man."

"Details, my arse!" McKeon roared.

"We'll settle this in an hour." McGarr glanced down at his fisherman's sweater. "And a half." It would be very pleasant to take a shower and change clothes. By the time he got to the office, McKeon would be so immersed in the details of this and other assignments he wouldn't even remember the outburst.

As McGarr made for the door, Horrigan said, "Wait —there's something I've got to ask you. How do you feel about the IRA?"

Now it was McGarr who was taken by surprise. He wondered why this question, why now. "I don't understand."

"You see, if you do manage to find the report before it's released to the press, then—well—I must know if—"

In that light, the question seemed innocent enough. After all, Horrigan had his entire public career on the line. As Horrigan himself had said, McGarr repeated, "I support the IRA."

"Well—how much, you know, theoretically?"

"Right down the line. Some tactics, of course, I deplore. For instance, the bombing of any target other than military. Cops are paid to take their chances. But as for the violence itself, have they any option?"

Horrigan smiled and nodded. "Oh, and here." He reached into his suit-coat pocket and drew out what looked like a bank cashier's check. Face side down he held it out to McGarr. "Just to reimburse you and your wife for having gone out of your way to meet me here today, and for whatever additional burden my wife and family will put on you during the course of this thing. Please don't mistake me, it's only a harmless gesture."

McGarr, who had grasped the check, released it and drew his hand away. "No need—I'm paid to be of assistance to all Irish citizens. Perhaps not well enough, but that's a bargain between me and the state." McGarr left.

4

McGarr's Dublin Castle office had not been designed for the baker's-dozen detectives who comprised his staff. Nor had the builder considered the possibility that persons other than mild British civil servants with low voices and an ease of manner might people these rooms. When the number of detectives not away on assignment rose above six, the main room teemed with activity, the clacking of typewriters, ringing of phones, citizens with complaints or information pushing close to a detective so as not to be overheard.

After hanging up his hat and coat, McGarr signaled to Hughie Ward. He already knew what Ward would divulge but planned to act surprised, if only to make the young man think his work had not been in vain.

Into the closing door of the cubicle, McGarr heard McKeon say, "More smoke and shadow! This place will be a bloody fen before our roving Inter-po-lice man gets through." McGarr's staff was very proud that their chief had been one of the most prominent international detectives in the world.

Ward sat on the edge of McGarr's desk and said in

a low voice, "Leona Horrigan is her name."

"Not—?"

Ward nodded. "The minister's wife."

McGarr pretended to ponder the fact. "Where's Brud Clare now?"

"Back at the boatyard."

"Did you make sure he understood how sensitive our investigation here has now become?"

Ward nodded again.

"Send in Slattery, then swear out arrest warrants for Hubbard and her. You can call her address the Shelbourne, for form's sake, and his Fitzwilliam Square. I don't know the number. You better check to see if he's an alien. If he is, notify the British Embassy."

"Then what?"

"Wait for me."

Slattery's inquiries at lawyer Greaney's had resulted in the name, Cobh Condominia Ltd., a holding company. The law clerk at the office refused to tell Slattery who owned the company or if it held title on other property than the 17 Percy Place address. Slattery had insisted on seeing Greaney himself, who told the detective he'd need a magistrate's order before he would reveal more.

"Get it and get the information. I want to know the name of everybody involved with that property and a list of the company's holdings. Then I want you to take every person concerned and run their finances down. Greaney himself included. Seems to me he's not the sort of lawyer that people operating aboveboard usually retain."

McGarr then called in Harry Greaves, who said the canvassing of Killiney hill was half completed without a witness having been discovered yet.

McGarr placed a call to Hugh Madigan in London, who corroborated Horrigan's story. McGarr couldn't extract any additional information, but got the impression Madigan wouldn't accept another assignment from Horrigan.

"Did he pay you?"

"Yes—promptly and in full."

"Then what's the problem?"

"I couldn't tell you without betraying the confidence of my client. You wouldn't want me to do that, Peter."

"Not often. But in this case it would be extremely helpful."

Madigan paused for a while.

Vaguely, beyond the line static, McGarr could hear other telephone conversations, the voices layered over each other so that only a word or two became intelligible now and then.

"I wouldn't be a friend unless I told you to watch out for the man. He's unpredictable and utterly ruthless."

McGarr had just put the phone down when it rang. Paul Sinclair, who was staking out the Percy Place apartment, had observed a tall, striking woman in her thirties enter the premises. Being alone, he could only cover one entrance.

"Hair?"

"Black."

"Built?"

"Like a pregnant kangaroo."

"How's that?"

"She had on a fur coat. In such important matters I dare not trust my imagination."

From the speed with which McGarr grabbed his hat and coat, the office staff knew this was no time to fool.

Ward was holding the door for him and they rushed down the stairs into the courtyard. Ward switched on the lamp and the bell, and they raced down Dame Street.

Trinity College students, having just returned from summer vacation, were flooding across Parnell Square toward the university gates. Blue-and-grey mufflers were wrapped about their necks. Most of the men were incredibly hairy and many smoked pipes. The gait of the women held a promise, just the slightest lubricity of young hips, that McGarr found disconcertingly attractive.

This scene, however, had exactly the opposite effect on Hughie Ward. He pumped the brakes, pounded the heel of his fist into the horn button, and shouted, "You blasted lard arses! Can't you see we're in a rush? Move it, idjits!"—which just caused the students to slow their pace yet more and assume an even more disdainful expression. Self-consciously anti-institutional as only the sons and daughters of the profoundly middle class can be, these kids seized any opportunity to bait society's most conspicuous institution, the police. McGarr was old and successful enough to find the stance ludicrous, but Ward was wroth.

He jammed the Rover into first and nearly burst the engine hurtling up Nassau Street. McGarr said nothing, just grasped the lid of his bowler and let his assistant sublimate his aggressions on the machine. A block and a half from the Percy Place address, McGarr reached over, silenced the bell, and switched off the light.

"She hasn't left by the front door. I did see the curtains move on the ground floor, however," said Sinclair, bending to speak into the front window of the car.

McGarr said, "You take the rear, Hughie. If you see her making off, don't wait for us. Suspicion of murder, high treason, grand theft, and violations of the arms-control bill are the charges."

McGarr popped out of the auto, and he and Sinclair hustled across the street. Sinclair was a tall, thin man who wore exquisite Savile Row suits, soft hats from Cavanaugh's, and carried an umbrella. He had been a full superintendent Down Under and was a member of the Australian Bar. He had the manner of a psychiatrist, and McGarr had strained his relations with the minister for finance getting the government to pay Sinclair only a hundred pounds per year less than he received himself, although by the rules of the Civil Service Commission that man's job classification could only be pegged at detective first class. McGarr was not afraid of competition, since he believed policemen, like athletes, could improve their game only with steady competition of a high order of excellence.

Sinclair rapped on the porter's door. A whole minute later, it opened.

McGarr pulled the arrest warrant from his raincoat pocket and attempted to show it to the old woman who called herself Megan. "Peter McGarr again, ma'am. This is Detective Sinclair."

The tall man was trying to see over the top of the old woman's head. They could hear the Rover winding down the alley out back.

"I seem to have misplaced my glasses," she said, but when she began fumbling with the shawl on her upper chest in search of her spectacles, McGarr pushed by her. He wasn't about to let any doddering old shrew keep him from making this arrest. He wanted to prove to the government that the Dublin Castle Garda had the tact and discretion to handle even the most sensitive assignment. Under other chiefs the Dublin Castle had been a meat-wagon squad that specialized in bullying, intimidation, and even torture. De Valera's regimes had used them for political purposes. McGarr had taken the job only on the promise he would be allowed to make the department into a first-rate investigative agency. Now he wanted to nip any political complications of this case in the bud. Arresting Leona Horrigan would be the first step.

"Where are you going? Two A has been declared void, you know," she shouted after him as he made a quick tour through her flat and opened the door that led up to the tenants' apartments. 2A was the Emergency Powers Act that had suspended civil liberties and had given the government the power of internment during the Troubles in the thirties. 2A hadn't been withdrawn, but the old woman's acquaintance with the law surprised McGarr.

The apartment was unoccupied, but the odor of a perfume that smelled like fresh gardenias was still heavy in the air. From the porch, McGarr signaled to Ward in the alley. He hadn't seen anybody leave. The back gate, however, was slightly ajar, as was a drawer of the dresser in the bedroom. Somebody had rifled through it, perhaps taking fresh clothes. A pair of women's shoes, the soles still wet from the street, were in the closet. McGarr slipped them into a paper bag he took from the bottom drawer of the fridge. He handed these to Sinclair, saying, "Have the lab check them for blood of Bobby Ovens' type, please, Paul. And then look up Liam O'Shaughnessy at the Department of Justice. He'll fill you in on the details of what he's doing. Tell him I told you to concentrate on Carleton Driver, the minister's first assistant." McGarr wanted his best men on that aspect of this investigation now, the two parts of which he was sure would dovetail very soon.

Sinclair left.

Back in the car, Ward asked, "Where to?"

This was no time for a long shot, but McGarr said, "The Killiney Bay Yacht Club. I have a hunch she's panicked. If so, she'll run to Hubbard. The old woman probably told her about my earlier visit, pointed Sinclair out to her."

As Ward cranked up the Rover, again sounding the alarm and activating the blinker, McGarr called Will Hare at Internal Security and John Gallagher at Customs, asking them to detain anybody named or resembling Leona Horrigan.

Gallagher asked, "Is that *the* Leona Horrigan, the minister's wife?"

"The same."

"And a prime piece of fluff she is," said Gallagher. "What's she done? A crime of passion, no doubt."

Ward began to laugh. Gallagher was a free spirit. Anybody with a citizen's band radio could be listening to them, to say nothing of all the police cars and station commanders across the country.

"We went to university together," Gallagher went on. "She had a certain way of tossing her hair, you know, that made me want to commit a mortal sin. She was"— they could hear Gallagher sigh—"the Lauren Bacall of UCD, but healthier, if you know what I mean. Nicotine could never violate those lungs!" Gallagher rang off.

Topping Killiney hill at the Khyber Pass, McGarr noticed the yacht-club van parked near the entrance to the lounge bar. He stifled the bell, turned off the light, and directed Ward to swing around.

When they got to the bar, McGarr noticed a neat whiskey and one with soda in front of adjoining stools. A cigarette with a lipstick smudge on the filter smoked in the ashtray. McGarr flashed his shield at the barman, who pointed in two directions, toward the men's room and out the front door.

McGarr took the former path and burst into the toilet. Along the outer wall, a bank of windows was open, the floor still wet, air heavy with chemical cleanser. McGarr was about to squeeze under a window and reconnoiter the yard beyond when he noticed the tracks of rubber-soled shoes leading to a stall. He could not, however, see feet below the door. He drew his Walther, and with a snap of his knee thrust a heavy-lidded wastepaper basket over the tiles so that it crashed into the stall door, jamming it open. There, squatting with his feet on the bowl rim, was Horace C. K. Hubbard. He looked very much like a frog on a rock.

"Who am I to question your toilet training, Horace? Climb down off there, please. Then come out here and place your hands on the wall."

From outside in the parking lot they heard the soft thump of automobile sheet metal collapsing, then the tinkling spray of shattered glass.

Hubbard shouted "Lea!" and made as though he would charge out of the toilet.

McGarr shoved the large man against the wall. Hubbard spun and punched wildly at McGarr's head, knocking off his hat. The chief inspector followed the arc of Hubbard's arm, and when the elbow swept past, McGarr thrust his weight into it. Hubbard's fist smashed full force into the wall tiling of the toilet.

Through the elbow McGarr could feel Hubbard's wrist snap. The big man pulled the hand back from the wall and stared into it curiously as it dangled limp, the knuckles bluing, the swelling immediate and full. He looked at McGarr as though for a diagnosis.

"You won't be thumbing your nose at me for a while, Horace," said McGarr.

Leona Horrigan was unhurt. She was indeed beautiful. She clung to Ward as though even in her collapse and embarrassment she was attempting to use her glorious body—a tall woman with straight, athletic legs and an erect carriage that emphasized her firm buttocks and large breasts—to win over the handsome young detective. She was sobbing, and like a child who derives emotional support from a teddy bear, wouldn't release Ward, who said to McGarr in a hushed voice, "And who said this job doesn't have its moments?"

McGarr directed the three of them into the rear seat of the Rover and drove to the hospital himself. The radiator of the car was leaking some, but the engine didn't overheat. He called the Bray barracks for help at the hospital. McGarr enjoyed the heady aroma of gardenias and the spectacle of Hubbard in agony, the woman mortified.

While the emergency room ministered to Hubbard's needs, McGarr made a discreet inquiry as to Ovens' condition, which had improved so significantly that Dr. O'Higgins was contemplating releasing him. The young doctor, McGarr found, was scheduled for ward duty that night. This bit of news pleased him, although the ward report said Ovens had not said a word yet. He had persistently refused to talk to the doctors, nurses, sisters, and priest.

Hubbard's fingerprints were on the winch handle along with those of another man. McGarr swiveled in his chair and looked out the window. The dirty brick buildings that bordered the Liffey appeared crimson as an autumn twilight descended. He picked up the telephone and began dialing the pubs he suspected Billy Martin might frequent. At the ninth, he reached a publican who had just seen the man leave. He advised McGarr to wait five minutes and then call Pim's Lounge Bar on the Stillorgan Road. "You can set your watch by the man. He rides a mo-ped, you know. Takes it right up on the sidewalk when the traffic's jammed."

While he waited, McGarr called Noreen, filled her in on the details, and advised her he wouldn't be home.

"Shall I pack up your dinner and bring it down?"

McGarr knew Noreen would do anything to get in on the interrogative aspects of an investigation. He could see Kevin Slattery at his desk, also on the horn to his missus, making excuses why he wouldn't be home. Slattery was the stenographer for interrogations. "What are we having?"

"Curried prawns on wild rice. How many are there of you?"

"Well, if you come down, I could send Kevin home, so that would make just Hughie, myself, and Mrs. Horrigan and you. We'll let Hubbard eat prison food."

"One hour." Noreen hung up.

McGarr pointed to the door. Slattery smiled and left. Thus, the department wouldn't have to bear the expense of having a matron in the room while Mrs. Horrigan was being questioned.

Billy Martin told McGarr that yes, before McGarr had arrived at the yacht club, he had touched the winch handle.

"Whereabouts?"

"Two places, I believe. The handle itself, you know. And then, because it felt so slimy what with his brains on it and all, I lifted it up by the base to get a better look."

"Why didn't you tell me that at the scene?"

"You never asked, for one. For another, you seemed so concerned that I not touch it, I figured that as long as we was drinking together, I'd not destroy the moment with such an admission. I should have known better. How's it coming, sorr? Do you still think it wasn't an accident?"

"Did you see a woman around the boat at all Friday afternoon?"

"Like I said before, Inspector, I never saw a woman around that boat. But then, I'm not of an age that I'm exactly looking for them, don't you know. Recently, I've been poking around the boat, sort of tidying things up for the unfortunate man. Is that all right?"

"Yes."

"And I've come across some fancy duds, the like of which a woman would wear, so I believe the man did dally with the creatures at one time."

McGarr wondered why Martin hadn't seen or wasn't telling him he had seen Leona Horrigan on the dock that afternoon. "How's your eyesight, Billy?"

"Not bad at all, at all."

"Ovens had your tools, didn't he, Billy?" McGarr had a report on his desk listing the contents in the garage that the sailor had used as his work shed. Most of the tools had "Mairtín," the Gaelic spelling of the surname Martin, either burnt into the handles or engraved in the metal. Clare had implied that once the debt on *Virelay* had been paid off, Ovens did no more work on the furniture he had been making in the shed. That meant Martin had known Ovens well enough to lend him his tools before Ovens took *Virelay* to Killiney Bay Yacht Club. Also, the Dun Laoghaire barracks of the Garda had sent McGarr a memo stating Martin had tried three times to get into the garage over the weekend.

"Again, sorr, you never asked. I tried to be as helpful as I could, remember? I'm not a cop. So much more the shame."

That was exactly the phrase Megan had used, but it was not unusual among older people.

"Well, I am. How long had you known Bobby Ovens before he put in at the club?"

"Certainly, sir, you don't suspect me? About six months. We're both boating people, don't you know. We both like a jar or two from time to time. It was only natural that I ran into him."

"Was—*is* Horace Hubbard in love with Leona Horrigan?"

"Who?"

"The minister for justice's wife, Leona Horrigan. Surely you know her. She's a member of the club, has at least two boats moored there."

"I don't think a blimp like him would stand a chance with a well-placed and luvelly lady like her."

"Did Bobby Ovens owe you money?"

"Me?" Martin began to laugh.

"Do you now or have you ever belonged to the IRA or any of its affiliate organizations?"

"No. I once belonged to the IRB, way back when I was in my teens. But I joined the Fianna Fail early on and resigned the Brotherhood when Dev. sidestepped the Oath to the Crown and took his seat in the Dail. Dev. was the man for me, always."

"I can check on that."

"Do. How's the poor blighter coming along anyhow?"

"The hospital lists him as dead. I'm waiting for a report from the pathologist now."

"Ah, God." And then without so much as a pause, he added, "Since you know my habits, stop around for a pint after work, sir."

"Perhaps one of these days, Billy. Answer me a final question—why didn't you tell me about the siren going off right after Ovens fell into the water?"

"Sure and I've worked at the club for years, Inspector, and the bloody thing goes off so often I don't hear it much anymore. But now that you mention it, it did go off. I must have forgotten about it. A crippled chap up on the hill runs it. His name is Moran. He's a club member too. He's got a pair of Jap binos through which, some claim, he can see London."

Noreen arrived with their supper and Hughie Ward, who had nipped out for a tête-à-tête with Sheila Byrne, had returned in time to ask Leona Horrigan if she would dine with them in the day room.

McGarr called Horrigan in Naas, then at the Shelbourne, and finally reached him at his office in the Department of Justice. He told him about his wife's detention. The minister seemed pleased that McGarr had moved so fast. He claimed to know nothing of Hubbard, and even the name was unfamiliar to him. "Is he her latest?"

"I don't know." Leona Horrigan's social life was none of McGarr's business.

"Are you going to make a charge against her? Shall I contact a solicitor?"

"I won't press anything without contacting you first. I'm not sure of anything. They both ran, however."

"Please keep me informed, Peter. Your assistant, Superintendent O'Shaughnessy, would like to have a word with you."

"Would you have him call me in a half hour? I'm just about to eat." McGarr preferred to speak to O'Shaughnessy beyond Horrigan's hearing.

Before he could walk out to the day room, where Noreen had set the center table, the laboratory called. Al McAndrew, the chief chemist, had found blood spatters of the same type as Ovens' on the shoes McGarr had lifted from Leona Horrigan's closet. The spots were about three days old.

Ward returned from the detention block to say that Mrs. Horrigan had already eaten with the other prisoners and wasn't hungry. McGarr sat and, as he ate, began leafing through the dossier Ward had compiled about Horace C. K. Hubbard.

He had graduated from St. Columba's College, a secondary school in Rathfarnum, and then Trinity College, Dublin, where he had read philosophy under Dr. Luce and had received first-class honors. In his final year he had published the paper "Berkelian Elements in the Epistemology of Gustave Flaubert," which had been widely acclaimed. Twelve years later he was still listed as a research student at Trinity.

The pilaf was a delicate mélange of wild, brown, and Italian long-grain white rices baked in chicken broth and white wine. One of Noreen's specialties was a chutney—her grandfather served forty-seven years with the Grenadier Guards in India—the sweet and pungent spices of which made McGarr's nose sweat. This was a sure sign the food pleased him. Dublin Bay prawns in a mild curry sauce was one of his favorite dishes.

The phone rang. Ward got up to answer it.

Hubbard, as he had said, did live on Fitzwilliam Square, but no thanks to his own efforts in the world. The house had been left him by his maternal grandmother, whose husband's name had been Farrington-Smythe. The taxes had been in arrears, and the bailiff had nearly auctioned the premises when Hubbard came up with a check covering what was due as well as the current year's assessments.

That windfall dated from the time during which he was "reading" at the British Museum for his Ph.D. thesis, which he was calling "The Decline of Metaphysical Language in the Seventeenth Century." His new tutor, Mr. J. P. G. Gomes, believed Hubbard to be brilliant and predicted his thesis, which Macmillan planned to issue in the spring of 1976, would be an intellectual event of no slight significance. Gomes opined that the man's politics had a Marxist orientation, "as is often the case with people who have inherited their money." The British Army had cashiered Hubbard for being a homosexual.

That stopped McGarr.

Ward entered the room. O'Shaughnessy was on the line.

"It looks like Carleton Driver is our man. Didn't show up at work Friday morning, which isn't unusual when he's on the booze, but he never put in an appearance at McDaid's all Friday, Saturday, Sunday, and today, which is something of a record around here. No work today either." McGarr could barely hear him above the din in the barroom. "Sinclair's running him down right now. Brian Coffey poked around Neila Monahan's place. The old girl hits the sack around eight and reads. An even older crone saw her in bed at fifteen-minute intervals right up until twelve-forty-five when the light went out. Shall I notify the Vice Squad?"

"Where are you headed now?"

"Home to bed."

"Could you stay there for a bit? Have a jar or two. Hughie will be by with a writ to search Hubbard's house in Fitzwilliam Square. I want you to look for any evidence connecting him with a group that might want to lay hands on the papers. Also, keep an eye out for anything that might involve him in the Ovens affair—love letters, correspondence, personal stuff. I'm reading a report that says he's queer, so don't look just for female stuff."

"Is Ovens a fairy too?"

"Never thought of that."

"What's happening there?"

"We collared Horrigan's wife. She had Ovens' blood on a pair of shoes."

"This Driver fellow was often seen with a tall, handsome woman who picked up his tabs. She didn't call herself Horrigan, though. Will you be there all night?"

"Think so. Anything else?"

"She could and usually did drink him under the table."

McGarr hung up, dialed the Customs night superintendent, and rescinded Billy Martin's travel privileges. He then called young Dr. O'Higgins and told him what he wanted. The physician objected but McGarr assured him Ward would use an ambulance and a certified police surgeon. McGarr handed Ward the writ O'Shaughnessy needed and asked him to drop it off on the way to the hospital.

McGarr swiveled in his chair and looked outside. The sky was black and a chill north wind quivered the glass shields of the street lamps.

Gerald, the gate guard, knocked on the door and then placed a brown bag filled with Harp lager bottles on the table. Noreen judiciously lowered it to the shadows beneath the table. Leona Horrigan was a felony suspect, but she was also the wife of the minister for justice.

McGarr began eating his dinner once more.

Hubbard had been engaged to be married once, but because of the discharge from the British Army, the girl's father broke off the engagement. Hubbard was fond of Irish wolfhounds, skeet shooting, and yachts of the size he could not afford without taking a job in the glass works his mother's side of the family ran out in Bray. Her brother—his uncle—had offered him a position on several occasions, and then, despairing, had disinherited Hubbard and offered company stock for public sale. Now Bord Failte owned a controlling interest in the business.

While McGarr was opening a bottle of beer to complete his repast, Bernie McKeon burst into the room flapping a large piece of photographic paper. He slapped it on the table. "Don't touch. Don't anybody touch that work of art, it's still wet. In police circles you could call it a Rembrandt or at least a Reynolds." McKeon was a small, muscular man with fair hair. Like most gentle men who join the police, his manner was self-consciously gruff. "And what have *you* been doing with yourself today, Chief Inspector of Detectives?" He was eyeing McGarr's bottle of lager.

"A little of this, a little of that," said McGarr, baiting him.

"And not without all the comforts of home!" McKeon lifted the lid of the chafing dish. There was still plenty left.

Noreen spooned some rice onto a plate and then added the prawns.

Said McGarr, "Let's see what you've got here, McKeon. Perhaps it might deserve a beer."

It was a blowup of the dock area of the Killiney Bay Yacht Club. Both Martin and Hubbard could be seen leading a woman away from *Virelay*. Although the enlargement was quite grainy, she had twisted her head back to the boat, as though looking over her shoulder. Her mouth was open in anguish. Ovens was still lying on the deck, dark splotches on the sail where his head rested. This meant that in two separate actions somebody had clubbed him and then, later, dumped him into the slip.

"Well?" McKeon demanded, hands on hips.

"Give him a beer," McGarr said. "But only one. He's an inside man and I doubt he could handle more."

"Hand me that bag, sonny!" McKeon demanded. He was two years older than McGarr.

After Bernie had eaten and Noreen had cleared the day-room table, a policewoman led Leona Horrigan into the room.

"Tea?" Noreen asked her.

She shook her head. Her eyes were worried.

"As you can see, we're also drinking beer. Does that bother you, Mrs. Horrigan?" McGarr asked.

She shook her head once more.

In a corner of the room, McKeon was sitting in one chair with his feet on another, a fat, green cigar clenched between his teeth, the beers lined up in rows not quite a reach from him. Noreen was seated at one end of the table. McGarr directed the Horrigan woman to the seat at the farther end.

McGarr noted that Leona Horrigan was the sort of beauty Irishmen think of as particularly ethnic when away from home. Her hair was so black and fine it hardly resembled hair at all, but rather tousled black down. Her skin was very white and eyes green. And she was a big woman in every way. "Does my husband know?" she asked. In the direct light from above her head, her prominent cheekbones shadowed her face.

McGarr nodded. "He knows you stole the Bombing Report."

She looked up at him. She blinked. For all McGarr could tell, she didn't know a thing about it. The words did not seem to register.

"You know—the little girl who had her leg blown off but she couldn't feel it was missing because her hand was gone too. The grandmother eleven times over—they buried what they could find of her. The Bombing Report!" McGarr almost yelled. "The one that covers for your friends you spent forty-seven thousand pounds on last year. The one that's going to hound the husband you hate right out of office!"

His tone frightened her, he could tell, but she hadn't stolen the report and probably didn't know more than what he had just told her.

For the sake of form, he said, "Shall we contact Solicitor Greaney for you, Mrs. Horrigan?" He signaled to Noreen to begin the record of their exchange at this point, since, if the woman were to be brought to trial for complicity in the Ovens attack, there was no need to have the report material available to the defense.

"Who?"

"Greaney, the solicitor on Leeson Street, the one who represents so many unsavory characters from North Dublin, the Vale Avoca Combine that failed, the Cornfeld mutual fund that bilked all the pensioners of their life savings, and also an outfit called the Cobh Condominia Limited of Seventeen Percy Place, Dublin. Do you understand me thoroughly now, Mrs. Horrigan? Do you want Detective Sergeant McKeon to stir Solicitor Greaney from whatever fiduciary miasma his mind is currently charting and include him among us tonight?"

She shook her head.

Very softly, McGarr added, "If you want a solicitor, if you believe you should have one here, tell us. We have no right to question you if you desire counsel and until he is present. That's the law."

She shook her head again. A tear had formed at the corner of her eye.

McGarr hated to admit it, but that the very sound of his voice had made such an extraordinary woman cry rather excited him. She had the sort of beauty he would like to crush.

"Now then," he said in the same mild voice, "I've read your dossier, spoken to your husband, have the reports of my staff concerning you, your activities here and in London and in the United States and on the Isle of Inishmore and with and without Bobby Ovens. You are an intelligent woman. No need—none," he barked, "for me to storm and shout at you all night tonight and all day tomorrow, and night and day in teams"—he pointed to McKeon—"until you admit to us what we already know. No need!

"Because I believe, Mrs. Horrigan, I can spare all of us that bother, because I believe you are, Mrs. Horrigan"—McGarr had put a foot on a chair near the one in which the minister's wife sat and was talking directly into her face—her bottom lip, crimson in the light, was trembling; in police work it was standard operating procedure to frighten those who could be frightened, and McGarr had succeeded with her—"a woman who wants to tell the truth. Everything I can read about you, all that people have told me about you points to that. So, let me tell you what I'm going to do." McGarr walked down to Noreen's end of the table and picked up his file of the Ovens case. Briefly he wondered if his allowing his wife to be present at a time such as this, his obvious enjoyment in grilling this woman in a brutal fashion, was some odd psychological foible of his. "I'm going to show you the hard evidence we have, and then let you tell me about it in your own words." He placed the still damp blowup of the photograph McKeon had found. "As you can see, that twisted bleeding man on the quarterdeck—"

"Don't." She averted her head and pushed the photograph from her.

McGarr waited for her to compose herself. "Your 'friends,' Horace Hubbard and the dock boy, Billy Martin, are there as well. They lied to me about you. Why would they lie to me about you? About what time was that?"

She was sobbing now. She shook her head.

"Now here we have a laboratory report about certain red spatters on a pair of white shoes you imprudently tried to conceal in the closet of your Seventeen Percy Place flat. Can you read it?"

She shook her head once more. Her eyes were brimming with tears.

"Shall I read it for you?"

She nodded.

"It says that's Bobby Ovens' blood on your shoes. Because the spotting is so regular over the surface of the shoes and the drops so tiny, it implies that you were within a foot of the man when the winch handle was being thwacked into his—"

"Stop!"

"Yes, stop it, Peter," Noreen said. "You're being barbarous."

"Well then, do you want to tell us about it, Mrs. Horrigan?" McGarr asked.

She firmed her bottom lip and looked up at him. The green of her eyes was bright through her tears. She had a mole the size of a threepenny bit at the base of her neck. The odor that rose from under the collar of her blouse was moist body and that damnably corrupt aroma of gardenias, heady, cloying.

"When did you first notice that Hubbard had the winch handle in his hand, when Ovens started up the companionway ladder? What part of it was he grasping, the arm or the handle? Did he throw it at him, or pick him up by the feet and swing his head into it?"

She shook her head. A tear caught in her hair and she pulled it away.

"Tell us about the sound of the blows."

She began sobbing.

"What was their effect? Were things suddenly, you know, mushy?"

She clasped her hands over her ears.

"And what did you do, Leona? Didn't you try to stop him, didn't you rush forward and grab hold of Hubbard's right arm?"

She was shaking her head.

"You mean you just stood back and let him kill Bobby Ovens?"

But again she shook her head. McGarr had gotten nowhere.

McKeon roared from the corner, "Goddammit, McGarr, let me question the *bitch!* She won't lie to me!" McKeon then knocked the accumulating empty beer bottles to the floor.

"Hubbard hated Ovens because the Yank was a better skipper," McGarr continued.

She nodded, then said, "No, no."

"What say?"

In a hoarse voice, Leona Horrigan said, "Yes—he hated Bobby Ovens. People will tell you that. But he didn't try to kill him. That's not like Horace at all. I—I realize I've been—incontinent with"—she glanced at Noreen, who, copying, had her gaze directed to the page of her pad—"men, but believe me, it's not because I want them fighting over me, it's because . . ."

"Because, because, because, because—it's because you're lying!" McKeon roared in the corner. "Goddammit, let me at her, McGarr!" His comments never appeared in the record. He was the vice. With other suspects his voice wheedled—"You look tired. Why don't you get it over with? A sympathetic judge and you'll be out in a year"—or coached—"Don't say a thing, don't give him nothing but your name and address. What would you want one of the others to do in your shoes? Sure—clam up and take eight years in Portaloise like a man? When you get out, they'll all have respectable businesses financed by your money and won't give you the time of day if you pass them in the street. Ex-con, but a tight mouth. Some men would consider the knowledge compensation enough.

You'll be able to hold your head high in the place of the odd publican who'll let you hang out waiting for whatever might drop from the sky in the way of a drink." His advice differed with every interrogation. McGarr thought him invaluable.

"Then Billy Martin did it?"

She didn't reply.

McGarr smirked. "What reason would Martin have for wanting to kill Ovens? They drank together. Martin couldn't have felt himself a rival for your affections, since he's old enough to be your father."

She looked up at McGarr, stared at him for a moment, and then said, "You don't know, do you?"

"Don't know what?" Bernie asked from the corner. "That one of your boyfriends is a fairy, the other a mouse, that you have to try to hurt the only strong man in your life, your husband? Eoin, your oldest son, told us the truth about you. He thinks you're strange."

She really was an intelligent woman and now realized what McKeon was doing. She said in a calm voice, "I'm not going to say any more. *All* these people are friends of mine."

"Even Bobby Ovens?"

"Especially Bobby Ovens."

"Did you sleep with him?"

Her head jerked up. With jaw firmly set, she said, "Yes. Often. Do you want to hear the details?"

"You slept with Carleton Driver."

"Yes—with him *and* with Bumpy Hubbard, and, if you like, I'll sleep with you too."

Noreen looked up from her pad.

"Do you—*did* you love all these men?"

"I don't know what that word means."

"Are you a nymphomaniac?"

"Yes!" She shook her head. "No. I don't know what that means either. That's none of your business."

"Do you drink?"

She lifted her head. "Do I want a beer? Yes—I want a beer."

McKeon stood, pried a cap off a bottle, and handed it to her.

"What's your opinion of Leona Horrigan?" McGarr asked her. He walked behind her chair to the door that opened into his office.

"Not much right now, if you must know." She sipped from the bottle.

McGarr opened the door. Ward wheeled Bobby Ovens into the room and positioned him right behind her.

McGarr said nothing, merely walked to the table and uncapped a lager. He wanted to see the expression on her face when she saw Ovens, whom she thought was dead.

After a while, she looked up from the table. A funnel of light shone on her limp hands. The rest of the room was in darkness. She glanced up at Noreen, who was staring beyond her shoulders, then at McGarr. He too was staring in back of her.

She turned. Ovens' head was still swathed in bandages, but he had a fresh cigarette in his mouth.

Her face softened dramatically. "Bobby!" she said and threw the chair back so it fell to the floor. She then fell to her knees and put her head in his lap. "They told me you were dead!"

Ovens merely drew on the cigarette and removed it from his mouth, staring at the wall over Noreen's head.

McGarr walked out of the room.

Five minutes later he sent Leona Horrigan back to her cell and tried to question Ovens. The man just smoked steadily, staring blankly off into space as though not hearing him. But McGarr was certain he did. McGarr didn't understand this curious character. He knew he could make use of the man's inscrutability, however.

He sent McKeon to fetch Hubbard from the detention block and sat him in front of Ovens, not more than six feet away. Ovens' haunting eyes, what Hubbard himself had described as "that damnable way of smoking and staring," began to work on the yacht-club steward. Even before McGarr had left the room, the bloated man had begun to squirm in his seat. "What's this all about?" he shouted after McGarr, as the chief inspector walked to his cubicle. "I want to call a solicitor."

"They tell me your credit isn't so good," said McKeon. "Whom do you suggest, Prince Hal? I'll only be too happy to call him. Or would you like to check with your comptroller first? We just returned her to her jail cell a moment ago. Beer?"

"Yes."

"How very Irish of you. Mr. Ovens, sad to relate, has requested the last bottle." McKeon uncapped the final two bottles. He handed one to Ovens, drank from the other himself quietly. The plan was to let Hubbard stew in Ovens' eyes.

5

McGarr dialed Hubbard's home phone and O'Shaughnessy answered. "Find anything?"

"Yup—in his study, third floor front."

McGarr waited. "Well?"

"Are you all tied up there, chief?"

"Not really."

"Then perhaps you'd better come down here alone. I don't quite know what to make of this."

"What is it?"

"A chart of some sort. And it's got names and places on it that have to do with both the Ovens and the Bombing Report cases. Murphy from Inishmore is on it, a fellow from Dun Laoghaire named Dalton. I don't exactly remember what your movements were over the weekend, Peter, but you had better take a look at it yourself. I don't like this thing one bit. It sort of smacks of a setup, if you know what I mean. It was left right out here in plain sight. He must have known we'd be looking the place over, so why didn't he destroy it? He's a weird bird, this Hubbard.

"Got a call from Sinclair. He's out in Naas now. A

Trinity student gave Driver a lift out there very late Thursday night or early Friday morning. Driver made the kid wait outside the hotel where Horrigan lives. Fifteen minutes later he rushed outside with two quarts of Bushmills. He thrust them at the kid, saying, 'One for either hand,' and then—get this—hopped in the minister's Bentley and drove off."

"How did the kid know it was the minister's Bentley?"

"That's a cute one, that is. The kid was the minister's son Owen. His father wasn't home but the door to the suite was open. The kid locked the door by pressing the button as he left. He said nothing seemed out of place, and it wasn't like his old man to leave the door unlocked or his car unlocked or his keys in the switch, so he started after the Bentley, since there was only one direction it could be headed on the road he had seen it take—over the Wicklow Hills toward Bray. But it had too much of a jump or turned off to Glendalough when young Horrigan chose the road toward the city. Didn't you have dinner with Noreen at the Royal Hotel in Glendalough on Thursday night?"

"Yes, we stayed late. Some of my mother's people live in Glen MacNass." It was the only public accommodation in the little village.

"That's what I thought. I don't care for this too much at all." O'Shaughnessy paused for a moment. "And then didn't you and Hughie Ward talk to a man at the Dolphin in Dun Laoghaire Saturday morning?"

"Yes."

"Did you go in there?"

"Yes. Why all the questions?"

"Only because the names on this list seem to follow your itinerary over the weekend. The name of the bookie shop next door to the Dolphin comes after that, then Murphy follows, then some Muldoon fellow in Belfast. You'd better come see this thing."

"Was Driver carrying anything other than the booze when he came out of the hotel in Naas? What did you say he looks like? Do you know if he always drinks Bushmills?" The stuff Horrigan had served McGarr had had a Bushmills smokiness about it, but McGarr couldn't be sure. Also, a tall man so skinny his shoulders had seemed mere hanging points for a drab raincoat had been drinking Bushmills at the bar of the Glendalough hotel. When McGarr had approached the bar to order a round they had swapped small talk about the weather. McGarr had taken only slight notice of the man except for the fact that he had specifically ordered Bushmills, a Northern drink not in great favor around Dublin. McGarr seemed to remember the man having a large blonding moustache and a face like Lytton Strachey, this is to say, like that of a malnourished horse.

O'Shaughnessy said, "The report is only ninety typewritten pages, small enough to fit under your belt. In his statement, the minister didn't say anything was missing but the report. It had been taken out of a briefcase that he had put in the sideboard. Driver is a tall man, slight, *with* a moustache. He's b—, ah . . ."

"Bald, go ahead."

"And has a limp."

The description fit the man at the Glendalough hotel perfectly.

"I don't know what he drinks besides quantities."

"Be there in ten minutes."

In passing, McGarr peeked into the day room. Ovens was still staring at Hubbard, who was now sweating copiously. McKeon had begun an explanation to Hubbard. "You see, you're the one being interrogated, so no brew for you, Hubbah. You might say you got jarred, then told us a pack of lies."

"Hubbar*d,*" Hubbard said. "I don't get 'jarred.' "

Noreen said to McKeon, "Give us a piece of the paper, Bernie." She switched on a light overhead.

"Tonight—you can count on it, Hubba*h,*" McKeon said to Hubbard. And then, skidding the front page of the paper across to Noreen, he added in a mock brogue, " 'Twas only an honest mistake. Muscha, the way the man pronounces his own name is meant for an Anglo-Irish ear alone, one that's within lip range, I should think."

McGarr decided to walk over to Fitzwilliam Square. There was something about a cold and wet fall night in Dublin that made the many pubs he passed seem inviting. Rainwater trickled icily through the chinks in the cobblestone streets and the brickwork sidewalks underfoot. The city's ancient stone had turned black, so that the yellow glow of the pub lights through leaded glass windows, some brightly colored, beckoned the passerby. When McGarr was astride a pub in King Street South, the door burst open as two patrons left and the sounds of the publican bidding them adieu, his other customers wrangling in low Dublinese, the heat, the tawdry odors of smoke and drink beckoned the chief inspector. He was half tempted to turn in for a pint. The barman had a face so creased and warted he looked like a reptile.

Hubbard's house, although one of the grandest in the entire town, was in surprising disrepair for the neighborhood. The brick façade badly needed painting. The mortar lines seemed to heave every which way, more like a fortuitous heap of rubble than a planned structure. The sashing needed replacement by a joiner experienced in fitting windows to old houses. On the third floor one pane was missing, a piece of cardboard having been taped over the aperture.

When O'Shaughnessy opened the door, McGarr said, "I wonder if the Gypsy lady is at home. I didn't see the red light out front, as described in your brochure, but I'm certain this is the place."

O'Shaughnessy shouted up the stairs, "A five-guinea high-roller coming up!"

McGarr saw a light go on in the house across the square. If Ireland could be said to have an upper middle class in an urban setting, here they resided. He began to sympathize with Hubbard somewhat, for he speculated this sempiternal graduate student was thoroughly hated by the denizens of Fitzwilliam Square.

And surely the house was just as McGarr had imagined it: an intellectual's lair. Columns of books snaked toward the ceilings as though Hubbard expected them to shore the crumbling edifice. He used paper plates in the kitchen and then burnt them in the fireplace, although his tastes ran to Continental delicacies—*escargots, salsiccia di cinghiale, caffè nero, bouillabaisse,* smoked herring and pickled onions from Holland. McGarr was pleased to see that he did indeed drink beer, Kirin from Japan. This made the chief inspector smirk and shake his head, for it was plainly an affectation. The rest of the world may have developed cuisines that surpassed Ireland's barely palatable cooking, but in McGarr's opinion, which he had garnered by means of the empirical method, the country produced some of the world's best beers.

He popped open a bottle of Kirin beer and immediately became yet more sympathetic to this fat, affected fairy. Kirin was smooth and bitter. The chief inspector had no qualms about nicking a drink from any house he was searching when the residents were away. He had early learned that the police would be blamed for taking something, so it was better to take something he liked. The cellar, O'Shaughnessy told him, was loaded with wines and brandies. Hubbard was not a property bourgeois, but rather a belly bourgeois, which made him only slightly more acceptable to McGarr.

For instance, upstairs, on the way to the study O'Shaughnessy had spoken of on the phone, McGarr looked in at the man's bedroom. It had a huge water bed that intrigued the chief inspector, since in the Dublin scheme of things bed was the place that the closing of the pubs forced a person to assume, and one's luck in the former institution directly influenced one's luck in the latter. Irish bedrooms were cold and a person needed all the heat he could muster for whatever purposes struck him.

O'Shaughnessy pointed to the top of a desk near the window with the pane missing. Under the glass surface protector was a chart, meticulously inscribed in india ink on oak tag. It read:

Driver
Horrigan—Naas, 24th Oct., '74
Dalton's for drop.
Murphy—Inishmore, 26th Oct., '74
Muldoon—Belfast, 27th Oct., '74
The Orangeman—(When required.).

The first thing that disturbed McGarr was the penmanship, the niggling way the serifs had been inscribed. This was not characteristic of the postgraduate scrawl he could see in the notebooks that covered the desk top. A man who undertook voluminous research and wrote long, complex books did not have time for the niceties of letter design.

McGarr picked up the phone and dialed his office. McKeon answered. "Give Slattery the assignment of learning who purchased oak tag—let's see, sheets about thirty-six inches by thirty-two inches—in the last week." There were only two shops in the city that sold oak tag. "In particular, have him take along photos of Hubbard, Leona Horrigan, Horrigan himself, and Driver, if you can find one. Maybe the clerks might recognize one of them. He can ignore any sales to the students of the College of Art."

"What are you onto?"

"I'll explain it afterwards. Call Spud Murphy's girl Eileen. Noreen will remember her last name. You can only rouse her on the wireless. The file in O'Shaughnessy's desk will tell you the call signals. Ask her to have Murphy get in touch with me by telephone. Insist upon that and tell her it's urgent. How's Hubbard?"

"We've had to call in some reinforcements to keep the lug on the hot seat. He tried to attack Ovens."

"Ovens all right?"

"He's a cool customer, that one. For all his inexpression, he evidently saw the attack coming and lashed out with his foot. Once—if you know what I mean. By the time I could react, Hubbard was on the floor rolling in pain and the Yank was still staring off into space, smoking his cigarette, drinking his beer."

McGarr was pleased to have his feeling corroborated that Ovens was indeed as fully conscious as he had ever been. From the way he had handled Hubbard he was obviously a man who must have been taken by surprise when he was attacked. If he had felt as much enmity for Hubbard as Hubbard for him, then he would have been wary of the yacht-club steward. Not so of Leona Horrigan, however, whose fingerprints weren't on the winch handle, or of Billy Martin, who seemed so ancient and harmless.

McGarr called McKeon back and told him to assign Harry Greaves the task of assembling a dossier on Billy Martin. Greaves was from Dun Laoghaire and his father, Harry, Sr., a retired foreman from the Port and Docks Authority. The older Greaves probably knew Martin personally.

O'Shaughnessy signaled McGarr over to the desk lamp. "Am I mistaken, or is this your home phone number?" On a scratch pad a near-dozen phone numbers had been scrawled. In fact, McGarr's was one. "Do you know this bird?"

"No."

"Did he ever have occasion to call you?" The Galwayman looked at McGarr suspiciously. "After all, it's no secret how you feel about the North and even the IRA." The Garda superintendent had served through the period when the IRA had sent roving assassination squads against the government police.

"You wore a sweater bulky enough to conceal the report, then stayed alone in Eileen's place, where you could have passed it to her or Murphy. Muldoon is probably Murphy's contact in Ulster." O'Shaughnessy did not make this statement in an accusatory way. He was just playing devil's advocate. Plainly, he was worried. This concatenation of near meetings, brushes in the night, phone calls, and so forth was too regular to be the work of McGarr. If the chief inspector had been a party to such a theft, certainly he would have taken pains to eliminate any trace of its disappearance. This was an inept trap that was being set for McGarr, but to those not acquainted with him and the worlds of police work and politics—say, for instance, a jury—a few more circumstances would make sufficient cause to press charges, if not convict. And charges alone would be enough to make McGarr's chief inspectorship, which he had held for a mere two years, untenable. McGarr may have been a fixture in international police work, but he wasn't as yet firmly established in Dublin.

The phone rang. It was Sinclair. He told McGarr he was in Glendalough. The barman at the Royal Hotel distinctly remembered McGarr standing alongside a man much taller than the chief inspector. "You see, the juxtaposition in your sizes was so comical."

"Your stint in Australia has given you such a way with words, Paul."

"To tell you the truth, I don't like the look of the Irish situation right now. Driver left a packet of matches on the bar that advertises a bookie shop in Dun Laoghaire."

"Dalton's?"

"The same. Something stinks here. I went to this Driver's flat. It's too neat for a drinking man, like somebody had just cleaned the place top to bottom, so I started searching the building. I found it strange that the trash bins were absolutely empty, this being a Tuesday before the Wednesday that the landlady said was collection day. She was sure she was full up, and when she took a look at the empty bins, she blew her top. They didn't belong to the premises at all, but she said she recognized their brown lids as those that belonged to a fish-and-chip shop down the street. There we found her barrels and in them I picked out a leather case. She swears it's Driver's. It's empty, but I called in a lab man and he believes it's got traces of greasepaint inside, you know, the kind actors wear. He won't know for sure until he gets it back to his microscope.

"Then nobody has really ever spoken to the man. He's a loner. They've heard him speak, mind you, ordering a drink or saying hello or when he's sloshed. Then he recites hours of verse in Gaelic or extemporaneous free verse in English that is often mistaken for babbling and with some justification. But nobody really knows him. This whole thing amazes me. I'll never sleep again." Sinclair, an insomniac, was unable to put his job aside.

McGarr thought for a moment. He had never known a heavy drinker, like Driver, to keep a neat apartment. Things got tossed about when a person was drunk. Drawers were left open, clothes got misplaced, food tins were left on the kitchen table, if the person thought of eating at all. "My bet is that somebody paid him to disappear and then went round to his digs and cleaned house. But, if he's got 'the failing' "—McGarr meant the man's obvious penchant for alcohol—"he'll eventually crave the company of kindred souls. Dropping out of sight for him probably means merely staying off the job and away from McDaid's. Where would a bloke like him go if he went on a toot?"

"Neary's, Molloy's, the bars around the theatres and the colleges. Any place where actors and writers hang out."

"He may be in disguise, however, given the grease-paint in that kit. But the one thing he can't disguise is his height, Paul. If he's the same man as the one at the bar in Glendalough, he's a giant and as thin as a rail.

"Also, tomorrow very early, I want you to roust out this Dalton fellow and, if he isn't utterly candid with you, collar him."

"What charge?"

"Suspicion."

"Suspicion of what?" The government, in particular Minister for Justice Horrigan, wanted the Garda Soichana to soft-pedal that charge. It had been much abused in the past when dealing with the IRA.

"Suspicion of trying to frame a chief inspector. I don't know. Suspicion of failing to pay his rates. Make something up, but find out how he fits into this thing. Every bit of it is too regular. It's a setup."

McGarr put down the phone, then picked it up again and began dialing.

"Who are you calling now?"

"Horrigan."

"This late?" It was a quarter to one.

"I hope he's sound asleep," said McGarr. All McGarr had as proof that the Bombing Report had been stolen was Horrigan's word, the word of a man whose wife had been involved in an attempted murder, a man who in the past had proved to be as ruthless and as personally ambitious as anybody in Irish politics. Horrigan wouldn't be acting out of character to have dreamed up the theft of the report and dropped several dozen clues pointing to McGarr, just to have something on him in case the chief inspector planned to lodge charges against his wife.

Horrigan wasn't in his office or at the Shelbourne,

but out in Naas. "Yes, Peter." He had been waiting right by the phone.

McGarr tried to make his voice sound perfectly official and correct, as if the investigation were right on target but proceeding slowly. "Just my final report of the night, Mr. Minister. I thought perhaps you'd be waiting for me to call."

"Yes, I was."

"We're close to forming some conclusions about the theft of the report. Driver did the actual stealing, but we have developed a whole avenue of investigation that won't come into focus until tomorrow." McGarr didn't want Horrigan to think he was putting him on and not telling him that they had found certain of the leads he had left. But, then again, he didn't want to alarm the man. Somehow, Horrigan had to plant some incriminating evidence on McGarr himself, say, for instance, the report or a copy of it. This, then, another branch of the police, perhaps Internal Security, would be told where and how to find. McGarr's idea was to catch Horrigan or one of his minions in the act of setting this last aspect of the trap. "I'll keep in touch."

"Thank you very much for your consideration, Peter. How's my wife?"

"Innocent, I believe. But I must prove it, since we've developed enough circumstantial evidence that a prosecutor not partial to David Horrigan's politics might make a very good case against her."

"What charge?"

"Complicity to commit murder."

"A felony," Horrigan mused.

"And then there are other details that might prove embarrassing. I'm currently standing in Horace Hubbard's study. That's one of the buildings which Cobh

Condominia Limited doesn't exactly own on paper." McGarr wanted to see if Horrigan would recognize the name.

"I don't understand. Hubbard I know. What's this other thing?"

"It's not important. Your wife paid Hubbard's rates, which had been in arrears."

"Oh."

"One other thing strikes me, sir. Why is it you called me about the matter we discussed yesterday and not Internal Security? It really is a matter for them."

"Well"—Horrigan paused—"I suspected Leona was involved somehow with Ovens and his misfortune, which you were handling, and also I don't know if you're aware of the part Internal Security played in the investigation of my involvement in the Bantry Bay oil farm many years ago."

"I was in France at the time."

"Suffice it to say, once bitten twice shy."

"Until tomorrow then, sir."

"Thank you again, Peter."

When McGarr replaced the receiver, O'Shaughnessy opined, "The bastard!"

"Right on the button, Liam. How are you feeling?"

"Wide awake and hot as Hades. Somebody ought to plug the son—"

"Would you do me a personal favor and drive out to Naas? I want you to shadow that guy. If he has people working for him, call the department and get some help. We'll see if we can make him move tomorrow. If we can just catch him when he tries to put the stuff on me."

O'Shaughnessy said, "But doesn't he realize that Sinclair and I and Ward and McKeon and maybe some others know all about this investigation?"

"He's counting either on your loyalty to me, in case I buckle and consent to quash the Ovens investigation in return for his overlooking my theft of the Bombing Report, or, if I don't, your natural desire to take my position. If I go, then everybody on this investigation team will be bumped up a notch in the department hierarchy."

"There's no humanity in that kind of thinking."

McGarr shook his head. "Plenty of his kind."

"You'll never find Driver. Horrigan is too rich and powerful for that. He'll buy him off or have him killed. I'll lay forty years in this racket on the line that says Horrigan would murder Driver himself to cover every eventuality. No passions or vices has that man—not booze, not women, not horses, gambling, not even tobacco. Just power. And you're just a pawn to keep his name out of the papers."

McGarr shook his head and slipped the piece of paper in his pocket. "I'm not sure you're right, Liam. There's something more here. It's not just his political career."

In a state of deep thought that made him oblivious to the driving wind and rain, McGarr left Hubbard's Fitzwilliam Square premises and walked back toward the office.

McGarr was confused. On the basis of circumstantial evidence alone, McGarr had enough on Hubbard to secure an indictment of attempted murder: Hubbard's fingerprints were on the winch handle; he had a grudge against Ovens both because of Ovens' relationship with Leona Horrigan and Ovens' superior sailing skills; if Martin could be believed, Hubbard was alone with Ovens at the time of the attack. Why, then, if the incident were so clear-cut, would Horrigan try to influence the investigation of a man who was his wife's lover? Was he as much in the dark as McGarr himself, or was it really Leona Horrigan who had attacked the sailor? After all, Hubbard was a big man, and three blows from him with an object as sharp and heavy as the winch handle would inflict wounds more grievous than those Ovens had sustained. But maybe not, given the doctor's description of the injury. No matter who was responsible for the initial crime, however, McGarr still had to deal with what he suspected was Horrigan's ploy to compromise the effectiveness of his investigation. That had to be his first order of business.

Passing through the gate to the Castle, McGarr decided he would try to reason with Hubbard. Intellectuals weren't often cowed by histrionics. Staring at Ovens staring at him had probably softened up Hubbard enough anyhow.

McGarr didn't pause to take off his hat or coat. He walked straight into the day room, and, facing Ovens, said, "Look at me." The tone of his voice brooked no denial. "Goddammit, I said look at me!" Slowly, Ovens' eyes moved to him. "You don't seem to care who clubbed you, nobody else seems to care about you, but one very powerful man in this government cares so much about stopping the investigation that he's trying to put me in jail. Did he"—McGarr pointed at Hubbard—"club you with that winch handle? I think he did and we've got enough evidence right now to prove it."

Ovens merely raised the cigarette to his lips and drew on it.

"Tell him!" Hubbard bellowed and the Gardai stuffed him back into his seat.

"Well, if he won't, why don't you?" McGarr demanded of Hubbard.

"Because I don't *know* how it happened, as I told you in the very beginning. One of those other two did it, or somebody whom one of the others won't say they saw. Or maybe, as I, neither of them saw who did it."

"Could it have been Horrigan himself?"

"I don't know. I don't think so. I really don't know the man. And nobody could have left the dock without being seen."

"Martin?"

"Could be. I don't know any more about it than you."

McGarr's temper suddenly squalled. "Then who in the name of hell *did* club him! It wasn't an accident, you know. He got hit, fell on the deck, then somebody rolled him over the side. Look at this." McGarr palmed McKeon's photo enlargement off the table and slapped it onto Hubbard's knee. McGarr then removed his hat and coat. He smoothed the hair along the sides of his head, touched Noreen's shoulder as he went to the small table, where he opened two beers. In a mild voice, he said, "All right." He handed a beer to Hubbard, saying, "It isn't Japanese, but you'll like it." He put his hand in his pocket, walked to the window, and looked out.

He remembered Horrigan's statement about their both being from Swift's Dublin. The old dean of St. Patrick had seen the world as it is. He had employed irony to purge illusion. Many, and Horrigan was one, had mistaken his stance for misanthropy. Hubbard,

McGarr then decided, might respond to the truth. "Let me tell you what I've got here, ah—what can I call you?"

"Hubbard. *Mister* Hubbard." He wasn't going to give McGarr an inch.

"How's the beer?"

"Wet."

"You're in trouble. A magistrate would indict you tomorrow. Your fingerprints are on the winch handle. How did they get there?"

"I took it out of Lea's hand."

"Why aren't her prints on it? What was she doing with it?"

"Gloves. I don't know how she came to have hold of it, but she didn't hit him. *Did* she, Ovens?" Hubbard demanded of the Yank. When Ovens didn't reply, he added, "You'd think he'd at least exculpate her for all she's done for him."

McGarr, glancing at Ovens, thought he detected a wry glimmer in the man's eyes. "Where are the gloves?"

"Burnt them. I wanted to burn the shoes and dress too."

"Why?"

"So Leona wouldn't get involved and have Horrigan meddling in her affairs."

"You mean the ones in the North, the gunrunning, the rocket launchers and antipersonnel weaponry?"

"Precisely. He'd then have to do something, you know. And given the excuse, he'd go after Leona with vengeance. The man is vindictive and cruel."

"Where's the dress?"

"Horrigan's Shelbourne suite. I thought that would be the safest place to hide it. In her rush to get in and out without the maid seeing her, Leona forgot about the shoes."

Noreen's ballpoint pen darted over the surface of Slattery's shorthand notebook.

"That's a crime."

"You're not interested in that." Hubbard was still uncomfortable under Ovens' gaze.

McGarr motioned to Ward, who wheeled the man out of the room. "You were in love with Leona Horrigan at one time?"

"Am in love with Leona Horrigan." He stared directly at McGarr when saying this as though it were a statement he dared the detective to challenge.

Here, McGarr thought, was a man who for all his breeding and brains was unworldly. He probably actively encouraged Leona Horrigan to hurt him. That's what Ovens was to Hubbard, the person whose relationship with Leona Horrigan inflicted upon Hubbard the exquisite agony he desired.

"Were you jealous of Bobby Ovens?"

"I *am* terribly jealous of Bobby Ovens."

"Would you kill him?"

"If I thought it would solve Lea's fascination for cretins such as he."

McGarr furrowed his brow.

"She thinks he's sensitive. I know he's obtuse. Anyhow—"

McGarr still didn't say anything, so Hubbard completed his thought. "—in this day and age monogamy is passé. We all are attracted to several members of the opposite sex."

"Is Leona Horrigan a loose woman?"

Hubbard flushed. "How do you mean, 'loose'?"

"An easy lay. Maybe even a nymphomaniac."

"If you please, Inspector! Such drivel! That term is

anachronistic—Freud at his worst, unable to conceal his own shabby Viennese morality. Some people have sexual drives which differ from the norm."

"And Leona Horrigan's differ?"

"The herd mind establishes norms."

McGarr handed Hubbard a sheaf of papers. "This report says you're a fairy."

Hubbard placed the report on the table without looking at it. "The British Army. I joined the Paras as a spy. They never suspected me—Anglo-Irish, family has a long history of military service, public school, Trinity. I served three years with a spotless record. They grew suspicious when my brother was blown up laying a mine at Crumlin Road Prison gate. I fled. Their only possible recourse was to sully my record. I can assure you my sexual preferences are profoundly heterosexual."

"What do you make of this?" McGarr handed him the chart he had taken from the top of Hubbard's desk.

After scanning the sheet of oak tag he said, "Nothing. I recognize some of those names but not Dalton or Murphy, assuming the latter isn't one of the countless Murphys that I, as any Irishman, would know."

"Who's Muldoon?"

"A Provo contact and C/O Fourth District, Belfast. That's common knowledge. The address is that of a safehouse."

"Did you have an occasion to jot my home phone number down on a slip of paper by your phone at any time in the recent past?"

Hubbard was genuinely surprised. "*Your* phone number? At your *home?* With all due respect, Inspector, that's not likely."

McGarr showed him the slip of paper. "I took this

from the top of your desk. Can you tell me something about the other numbers?"

Hubbard studied the many numbers for a few seconds. "No. Nothing. What's this anyhow? Have you decided to plant evidence on me now that you know I wasn't involved in the other thing?" He had grown wary again. Thick brown eyebrows hooded his eyes.

McGarr took the piece of paper back. "Another beer?"

"If I can't leave this place." Hubbard began kneading the skin around the end of the cast on his forearm as if it were beginning to bother him.

"Have a beer first." There was no chance that Hubbard would be let go without a thorough grilling in which he would be asked to repeat the information he had given in his formal statement to McKeon on Saturday morning. Discrepancies would be thrown in his face, he would be asked if he had loved his mother. McGarr still considered him the prime suspect in the attempted murder of Ovens.

The phone was ringing in McGarr's cubicle.

Noreen was getting Hubbard another bottle of Harp.

Spud Murphy was on the line and corroborated Hubbard's information about Muldoon.

McGarr swiveled his chair so that he talked into a corner. With his hand cupped around the speaker of the phone his voice was no longer audible in the office, although Murphy could hear him well enough. McGarr only hoped a bored Castle switchboard operator wasn't on the line. "If, perchance, something happens to me here in Dublin, can you make me disappear?" McGarr would never consent to sitting back and letting Horrigan hang this phony charge on him.

And only if McGarr were free could he prove Horrigan had fabricated the Bombing Report theft.

"Really? Not here. The place is too small, if you know what I mean. Let me think. What's happening there? If you've decided to come over to us, it would be better for our organization to have you stay where you are. We haven't had a man in the Castle since Jim Crofton got picked up trying to smuggle that German agent out of the country during the war. What a coup to have you there and working with us!" The fisherman was beside himself with the prospect.

"I really don't think I'll have the choice. I can't explain the situation now." McGarr was thinking about the recent change in the government. It had happened through a fiat of obscure back-benchers in the Fianna Fail party. Like Horrigan, most either were known to be opportunists or were relatively new to elective office. Three of them had assumed ministerial portfolios. Certain of the papers had tried to explain the phenomenon by saying Dev.'s old boys were over the hill and it was time for them to step aside, but De Valera's own paper, the *Press*, had said what was troubling McGarr: men like Horrigan had not paid their political dues, had no proven track records to show the people, and had yet to be "constitutionalized," by which the paper meant to convey the idea that none had shown he would adhere to the rule of law in a crisis. "Maybe I'm being paranoid, but I think I might have to run to ground. Tomorrow."

"Do you know Dingle?"

"Vaguely. But the place is small, like Inishmore."

"More tourists, though, Paddies on holiday. Wear some bright clothes and carry a fistful of dollar bills. You'll never be seen. Kelly's is the name of the place."

"Half the people out there are named Kelly."

"You'll find it, I'm sure. He'll be expecting you, so don't talk to the barman. Be patient, since he'll do some checking before he recognizes you. But he can make you so inconspicuous you'll think you're one of the little people."

"I hope I won't be needing his services." McGarr thanked Murphy, then hung up.

He called Noreen into the office and explained the situation to her.

She said, "The important thing is to get a confession from one of those two. Then you'll have something to bargain with, if you want to bargain."

"Yeah—but I don't know that he'll play the card, if I don't or can't or, knowing what he's up to, won't implicate his wife in all of this."

"Nonsense. Regardless of what happens now, the man has a chance to expand his power base by sacking you and putting his own man in this spot."

McGarr hadn't thought of that. Horrigan, with the consent of the Taoseaich of course, would name McGarr's successor. McGarr couldn't go to any other minister either, since none would want to involve himself in the affairs of any other minister's department, especially Horrigan's. The man had the reputation for being a scrapper. Rumor had it that, in a political sense, even the Taoseaich himself was afraid of the man. "Well, why didn't the bastard just come out and fire me?"

"That would be too easy. O'Shaughnessy and Sinclair and McKeon and all the rest wouldn't know why. Have you thought of the possibility that this situation involving you is just part of a larger scheme? Why didn't Ovens talk? Why didn't the blows kill him?

Think of how all-powerful that man and his cronies would be with their own private police force."

"Yes, I have. The thing that bothers me is that I don't believe we'll ever be able to prove conclusively that either Leona Horrigan or Horace Hubbard is guilty of attacking Ovens, if they continue to hold out. A gifted prosecutor might make all this circumstantial evidence stick, but without Ovens' testimony the case against either of them is tenuous indeed. Of course, the misdemeanors of concealing evidence, hindering an investigation, and so forth are possibilities. But both are first offenders. They'd probably have the charges filed. Perhaps Martin"—McGarr thought of the frail old man, a pensioner who enjoyed the odd sup and pub-hopping—"but what motive would he have had? The Yank had been good to him, I saw so myself. They probably got on as famously as one might expect from Ovens."

Noreen slid off the desk on which she had been sitting. "Well, the way I see it is that you've got to *make* her guilty in the same way he's making you guilty of stealing the Bombing Report. We haven't got much time."

It was 2:45 A.M.

McGarr was shaking his head. "You know I don't operate that way. If this job is going to be political, I don't want it anyhow."

It was Noreen's turn to shake her head. Her curls were springy. She was worried, her fine features drawn taut. "You're talking to me now. We both know how much you wanted this position. I suspect your years in Interpol have spoiled you." In order to avoid the charge of meddling in the affairs of any nation, the International Police scrupulously avoided any case that smacked of politics. "We've talked about this before. Meeting another person in the street is a political act. Anyhow, one of them knows who did it, and I'm betting the woman will break. She's too emotional to hold out forever."

Noreen was right. McGarr sat up. Another thing occurred to him. "I've taken pains not to arouse Horrigan. It could be that he hasn't yet placed any incriminating evidence on me—either at the house or in this office. Could you go home and—?"

McGarr didn't have to explain the thought further. Noreen packed up her wicker basket, pulled on her belted raincoat, and got two Gardai, whom McGarr instructed to watch his house, to drive her home.

McGarr then called the night desk and asked the sergeant to put a Garda patrolman by his Cooper.

Calling Ward and McKeon into the cubicle, he shut the door and explained the situation. He asked Ward to search every inch of the office and make sure the report had not been smuggled in already. He also asked him to post himself on the door in the morning and let only staff in, requesting them to show the contents of all packages and submit to pat-down searches. Anybody who objected could take the day off. McGarr hated to show he distrusted his staff, but Horrigan or one of his minions might well plant the material on one of McGarr's men without that man's knowledge and then another policeman besides McGarr would become involved inextricably in the devious minister's plot.

6

And so the night passed in a flurry of questions, questions repeated, counter questions, accusations, threats, denials, and bursts of temper as McGarr and Bernie McKeon, spelled by Ward, grilled the two suspects. Twice McGarr thought he had Leona Horrigan on the point of admitting that Hubbard had attacked Ovens, but he had misjudged her. She was emotional but strong. She held out.

With the approach of day, the wind stopped suddenly. A soft drizzle began falling. From the day-room window, McGarr could see the Liffey. It was the color of milky tea. Two swans followed the tide toward O'Connell Bridge, pecking at a cow pie. The Guinness brewery was wrapped in the steam from its mashing tins.

At 6:10 McGarr called Delaney, who lived out in Enniskerry, and asked him to pick up Billy Martin on his way to work. He then called Sinclair's house to learn if he had checked in there yet. His wife said he had been gone all night and asked McGarr if police business had really caused his absence. They had six kids. His wife's physiognomy, what with the children, had suffered a radical decline. "Yes," said McGarr, "he's a dedicated and gifted policeman and I know he loves you very much." He almost added that the morrow might see her hubby in McGarr's seat but said, "The senior men have been up all night long, Frances," and rang off.

Shortly after 7:00 the phone began answering back. The first call was from Harry Greaves, who was having breakfast with his father in the old man's kitchen in Dun Laoghaire. Harry, Sr., came on the wire. "Peter, boy, how's by you?" Well into retirement, the old fellow was still sharp.

"Billy Martin, Harry. What can you tell me about him?"

Greaves had spent his lifetime on the docks in Dun Laoghaire, the quay side in Dublin. "Don't know much. He's not from these parts."

That was strange. McGarr could have sworn the man had a local accent.

"He claims to be from the south someplace, Cork, I think."

Leona Horrigan was from Cork. "Anything else?"

"I see him drinking with many old Fenians, the has-been crowd who still ask, 'Where were you during the Troubles?' of kids who were conversing with the Holy Ghost at the time. You know—porter-bottle revolutionaries."

Several minutes later Sinclair called from Dalton's turf-accounting shop in Dun Laoghaire. "Nothing here, Peter. Dalton was arrested three years ago on suspicion of being involved in a border incident. Some shooting occurred but nobody got hurt. Since then he's been inactive. Says he doesn't know Driver.

Knows Horrigan because he saw him steal a bicycle when they were kids."

"First name Seamus?"

"That's his brother."

"Put him on." McGarr used to throw rocks at Liffey barges with Seamus Dalton, who got killed serving with the UN Peace-Keeping Force in Cyprus during the sixties. "This is Peter McGarr, Mr. Dalton. Do you remember me?"

"Sort of, Inspector. My mother always told us you were a bad type."

"And she was right." McGarr's mind conjured the headlines that would soon be appearing in the papers. "Horrigan, the minister—what do you know about him?"

"Besides having been even worse company than you when we were kids, nothing."

"Did you see me in your shop Saturday morning?"

"Yes."

"What did you see?"

"You made a phone call."

"Was there anybody in the box before me?"

"Every tout in Dublin County, it seemed."

"But specifically, right before me."

"Well, we were so busy and usually I wouldn't have noticed, but some time before you used the thing, a bugger was in there for a half hour. He had been popping in and out of the bar all morning long. I only took notice of him because he was so drunk one of my men had to dial for him."

"Tall and skinny with a moustache?"

"Your man here asked me that already. I wouldn't swear to it but I can have the clerk who dialed for him call you back when he comes in."

"Did he write down the number he wanted your man to dial?"

"You'll have to ask him."

McGarr thanked Dalton and told Sinclair to call his wife while waiting for the clerk to arrive. He hung up.

With his lips, McGarr pulled a Woodbine from its packet. When he reached into his pocket to find his lighter, his car key jingled. That was when it occurred to McGarr that he had been too late in placing a guard on his auto. The possibilities that Horrigan or Driver might have slipped the Bombing Report into the Cooper were three in number: one, when he first spoke to Horrigan in Naas; two, at the hotel in Glendalough; and three, at the turf accountant's shop in Dun Laoghaire.

Liam O'Shaughnessy walked into the office. Through the open door of the cubicle McGarr signaled him. He wanted to have somebody along as a witness when he checked the car, which was parked out in the courtyard under the night gatekeeper's eye. It then dawned on McGarr that Horrigan had somehow managed to get past the gatekeeper on Saturday night, which meant either the guard was lax or in the service of the minister for justice. No matter Horrigan's position, he had no business in the Castle offices after hours and the gatekeeper should have told him so or called the chief of Internal Security to accompany Horrigan.

After Ward patted down O'Shaughnessy, the big man walked into the cubicle with a styrofoam cup of tea in either hand. Outside, the city had awakened and the morning rush of traffic along the quays had begun.

The phone rang.

It was Solicitor Greaney complaining about Inspector Slattery, who had disturbed him while he was entertaining guests last night, had awakened him this morning, and whom he had found in front of his office this morning. "What in the name of David Nelligan will it take to have you call off your hound?" Nelligan had been the most hated policeman in the modern history of the country.

"The names of the principals in Cobh Condominia Limited."

"William and Megan Martin."

That knocked McGarr back. He sat up and sipped from the cup of tea. The similarity of names could be a mere coincidence, but he doubted that. "Could you put Slattery on?"

"If you'll promise to call him off now."

"It's as good as done."

"Chief?" Slattery sounded tired.

O'Shaughnessy was dozing off. He had evidently gotten a fresh man to pick up his assignment of tailing Horrigan, who was at work by now.

"The oak tag."

"Your wife Noreen bought it. Three sheets. I called her just now to check. She made a poster for your niece's birthday, remember?"

McGarr remembered all too well.

"One sheet is left. One is missing. Noreen says there's no sign of a forced entry at your place."

McGarr forgot even to thank Slattery. He hung up. The situation looked very bad indeed. If Horrigan had gone to such lengths to plant the chart, certainly he had somewhere concealed the necessary evidence that would conclusively implicate McGarr. He again picked up the phone, this time to call John Gallagher.

O'Shaughnessy was nursing his tea, taking successive, quick sips to keep from falling asleep.

"Can you remember another detail about Leona Horrigan for me, John?"

"Any cute curve, every luscious line."

"Her maiden name."

"O'Brugha—a lovely Gaelic name."

"Oh." McGarr was dejected. "Thanks, John."

"What—did I say something wrong?"

"No. Thanks again." McGarr hung up. He said to O'Shaughnessy. "Leona Horrigan's maiden name is O'Brugha. I was hoping for a break in this case, you know, that maybe her maiden name might be Martin or something like that." He sank into the chair. The tea was little help. He was punchy.

O'Shaughnessy said, "Now that's a very rare name, that is. I know of many Brughas. Off hand, there's Cathal, Caitlin, and Noinan, but the only *O'*Brugha I ever ran up against was from Cork. You know who he was—the schoolteacher whom the bishop sacked for spreading all the 'Bolshie' ideas way back in the thirties, who was the 'dean' of the 'University of the Curragh' all through the forties?" O'Shaughnessy's euphemism referred to perhaps the most barbaric prison in all of Western Europe. There the Irish Free State under De Valera had tried to break the spirit of the IRA stalwarts. "He was a hard man—the hardest, they say, but, you know, something of an artist all the same."

"In what way?"

"Hell—Mairtín O'Brugha spent ten years as an Abbey player. You probably saw him many times yourself."

"Mairtín?" It was the name that had been inscribed on the handles of the tools Billy Martin had lent Ovens, it could well be the Gaelic equivalent of Martin's name, William and Megan Martin were probably husband and wife, and Mairtín might easily have been one of the many aliases O'Brugha had used when he had been on the run. McGarr stood. "Grab your hat. I don't think Delaney has collared him yet. Maybe we can get to him first. His habits are regular and he'll be at the club now. I'll drive. You get hold of Delaney and call him off. I'd prefer to talk to the man away from the Castle."

They were in the courtyard. McGarr decided to take a police car rather than his own auto, at which a patrolman, according to his orders, now stood. He didn't want anybody to think O'Shaughnessy had anything to do with Horrigan's setup. Very shortly, McGarr would need every friend inside the Castle he could muster.

Killincy Bay was socked in. The fog lay on the still water like tufts of cotton. Not a soul was in the clubhouse or on the docks. The boats rose lazily in the occasional swell. It was mid-morning.

The postman stopped his bicycle and told them Martin did not work on such days, that he walked up the beach as far as Bray and began his measured libations at the Harbour Bar. He speculated that Martin toured many of the older spots in Bray before taking up his usual pub route in Dalkey later in the day. "He's the man for the odd sup, you know," the postman added.

McGarr and O'Shaughnessy beat Martin to the pub. The Harbour was the ideal place for an interrogation —a low, cozy barroom with a gas fire in the hearth and a barman whose morning duties made him scarce.

Nets hung from the ceiling and nautical mementos—a harpoon, a lifebuoy from the *Hibernia,* ships in bottles, a capstan, wheels, even a bollard into which dart players had stuck their birds—decorated the walls and mantel. In deference to the setting, McGarr ordered rum, O'Shaughnessy his usual, malt.

It was as though Martin had been expecting them. He doffed his cap and raincoat and sat with them. "Soft weather, what?"

McGarr had finished his drink.

Martin took the glass behind the bar, poured another, one for himself, and looked at O'Shaughnessy.

"Powers."

The gas was hissing behind the grate, which warmed McGarr's back and made him feel suddenly tired.

When the old man, whose bald head had begun to wrinkle like that of a baby, sat, he said, "Who told you?"

McGarr shook his head. "Nobody. Seventeen Percy Place."

"Did you talk to Megan? I haven't seen her in years. How is she?"

"She didn't tell us a thing. It was Greaney."

"It was?" He was surprised. "And there I thought the name Cobh Condominia sufficiently grand to make anybody think some bloody cartel owned the place. Did you have to take Greaney to court to find out?"

"Only a writ."

"Jasus—I've been paying him a small fortune these many years to keep that quiet. We'll have to talk to him, we will." The old man had paid for the drinks with a fifty-pound note, which he had tossed casually on top of the bar.

"I believe you'll be doing your conversing with the legal profession from behind bars, Billy. Doesn't Horrigan call the shots?"

"Christ, he tried to call this one and look at the mess we're in! I advised him a year ago to dispose of the Yank in a safe manner, either to deport, shanghai, or put the bugger out of his misery. But no, David was jealous or something and wanted to learn what Leona and him had going. And don't be so sure about putting me in the can, son. Do you know about the Bombing Report business?"

McGarr nodded. "You'll have to plant it on me first."

Martin closed his eyes and smirked. "Ah, lad. It's already on you, I'm sure. We in the Army have been doing things like this for so long that you, one man with one wife and a small retinue of friends and associates, could never stymie us." Martin took a sip from his half pint of porter and looked about the empty bar.

Near the esplanade that ran the length of Bray beach, the number 45 bus, a blue-and-yellow hulk, lumbered to a stop and off-loaded a nanny with a small child.

McGarr said, "I thought you told me Dev. was the man for you?"

"He was, the poor old fool. But only for a time. His idealism was shallow, his thinking half-baked. Once in power he didn't really know what to do but stay in power. He had no social program, no political altruism. Let's face it, the man hadn't much of a mind. He couldn't lead the people out of poverty and international political oppression. He had a peasant's point of view. He went hat-in-hand to Lloyd George, and what have we got today—partition."

"Dev. didn't go to London to the treaty proceedings," said McGarr. "When those other men came back with it, he wanted to repudiate the thing."

O'Shaughnessy, who was a confirmed Fianna Fail supporter, added, "For a long time he wouldn't take the Oath of Allegiance to the Crown, wouldn't take his seat in the Dail. In fact, he really never *did* take the oath."

"Fook the oath! He eventually took the seat, suppressed the Army"—Martin meant the IRA—"and brought us nearly forty years of lip service to values which he refused to pursue. He allowed the gentry to retrench itself, big foreign money to buy up the country, the bunch of bastards in the North to make the Six Counties a police state more repressive than Outer Mongolia. All that will change and soon! This place"—he swept his hand—"will become the Irish Republic in more than name only! And the sort of social and economic system that obtained before the Norman invasion will again hold sway."

"Communism, you mean?" O'Shaughnessy asked.

"Not communism. Who the hell knows what that term means anymore? Economic integration is what we'll call it. We'll put an end to private property."

"How?" asked McGarr. "Britain will never allow it. We're a poor country of three million and they have over fifty. We're tied to them commercially, geographically. We couldn't hope to defend ourselves against an aggressor without their active aid and support. We speak *their* language."

"Don't remind me," said Martin.

McGarr added, "In order to achieve the goals of the original revolution, the ones that the dreamers in the Army envisioned as *their* Ireland, or now, what you're talking about, we'd need the sort of regime that Castro set up in Cuba. I wouldn't want to see that happen here."

"Nonsense—this is Ireland, not some sultry banana republic in the Caribbean. Our people have been politically astute for centuries. If you haven't noticed, the lion is now on its uppers more completely than it was during the Depression." The old man shook his head. "Wake up, boy. This time we're building broad support among third- and fourth-generation Irishmen in the States, some firm ties with other revolutionary groups around the world, and a good deal of money and arms. The political bosses over in Britain don't realize how little stomach their people will have for the type of campaign a Dublin government that does more than blind an eye to the activities of a rejuvenated and well-financed army can launch. I, for one, am sick of what's happening in the North. How about you, boys?"

Both McGarr and O'Shaughnessy, like most Irishmen, were sick of what had been happening there for the past three hundred years.

"The rest of the world is too, and nobody more than the average man in any English street. And the day of an invasion threat is over. Our friends in America, the same ones whom the British are depending on to bail out their economy, wouldn't stand for it." Martin drank up, stood, and pulled their glasses from them. He walked toward the bar.

When the old man returned with fresh drinks, McGarr asked, "So, how has it come to be that a man like Mairtín O'Brugha, the idealist and conscience of the IRA, has attempted to commit murder in his old age?"

"Attempted?" he asked.

"Ovens isn't dead. I only said that."

"But I called the hospital, notified a Protestant mortuary so at least the poor soul might be buried properly."

O'Shaughnessy snorted into his raised tumbler. "Smoke and shadow. We're pretty good at that as well, old man."

O'Brugha was stunned. "So—I botched the job thoroughly."

"Why didn't you use a gun?" asked McGarr. "Why did you choose to hit him while he was on his boat, and why did you use the winch handle?"

O'Brugha shrugged. "We were belowdecks at the time. I figured I'd sail the boat out a few miles that night and scuttle her. That way we wouldn't have a corpse to lug around and a boat to dispose of. Nobody would miss him or *Virelay*—suddenly both would be gone and that would be that."

"Who called us in the first place?" O'Shaughnessy asked.

"Don't know. Certainly not us, I mean, Leona, Horace, or I. The bloody whistle went off on the hill and we panicked. I figured the cripple was watching us through the glasses, so we'd better look like we were saving Ovens. I belted the bugger in the cabin, but he wouldn't go down and blundered up on deck. Did *he* say anything to you?"

McGarr shook his head.

"He's a good lad, but unpredictable. An American, you know. We need soldiers, like the ones in the twenties, the ones that humped fifteen years of solitary."

But McGarr was not convinced by this confession. O'Brugha himself was one of the stalwarts who had, in fact, humped fifteen years of solitary. He was well acquainted with the police, courts, and prisons. All McGarr had on him was the fingerprints on the winch handle, for which he had a plausible explanation. After all, he was the dock boy at the club and Moran had witnessed him saving Ovens. "Tell me about Leona."

The old man took a long drink from the glass of black porter. The buff-colored foam scudded his upper lip. He wiped it off with the back of his hand. "My grossest human failure. Ah—I had others, her mother, my father, my brother Mick, Willy O'Connell whom I left bleeding behind the waterworks in Derry after we walked into an ambush. We all have regrets about how we've treated people, I suppose.

"Leona was born when I was on active service in 1931. A month later I was lifted and then transferred North. No extradition, they just handed me over to the RUC. 'Cold storage,' they called it. I broke out, got to the border, had a few months of freedom, and got lifted again. And so it went for twenty years, in and out. Leona couldn't have had less of a father if I had been dead." He paused to turn his seat so that he could look at the gas fire in the grate as he spoke. "About her, Butler Yeats, who was a friend I seldom got to see, said, 'Maud Gonne was a beautiful woman in the tradition of Leona O'Brugha,' for you see"—the old man turned his head to McGarr, his eyes were now filling—"he saw how Leona's beauty was greater and would be more a curse than that other woman's had been to her.

"Up until she became a beautiful woman, Leona was carefree, a happy child. And then it was as though the mental Leona viewed every beautiful change in the physical Leona as perfidy. She became ashamed of the beauty that caused women and men alike to single her out, and she hated my wife and me as the authors of her malaise. She took to dressing in loose clothes, became a recluse down in Cobh, where my wife chose to live among her own people while I was incarcerated. And we were told by the friends with whom she lived while she went to university in Dublin that, although besieged by men, she dated few and remained terribly shy. That reticence, of course, only added to her charm.

"My God, I myself then saw how right Leona was. Her beauty was truly like an affliction or handicap. Once, while I was on the run, we went out walking together around the Botanical Gardens. Jasus, I felt like I was on the stage. Some son-of-a-bitch with a Mercedes automobile sent his chauffeur in to tell us his car was at our disposal, and I nearly shot the poor servant, his being dressed in high-cut boots and a dark uniform like a Garda and all.

"Horrigan, whom she married, not because of any great passion but because he was then innocuous and kind, told me she buried herself in housewifery, her kids, his career. But you see, the unfortunate woman was also cursed with a brilliant mind. Horrigan couldn't have made all that money by himself. He's shrewd, but after the initial pot out on the Bantry, she took over. Have you thoroughly investigated Cobh Condominia Limited?"

McGarr shook his head. Slattery was probably doing that now.

"It also owns three acres of Oxford Street over in London. And that's just one of the companies she set up. Last year, as dock boy at the Killiney Bay Yacht Club, I made over a hundred thousand pounds. For tax purposes she spreads the money out among her relatives and friends. There's nothing mean about that woman. I've always had a passion for cigars." The old man opened his tattered raincoat and pulled a brace of cigars from the pocket of his khaki shirt. "So now I indulge myself. It's my one concession to wealth." He handed a cigar to O'Shaughnessy, then one to McGarr —hand-rolled Havana-Havanas with *claro* wrappers and reeking of cedar. "Where was I?"

"Leona," said McGarr.

"Ah—yes, Leona." He bit the nib off the end of the cigar. "As long as the cat's out of the bag I may as well smoke in public." O'Shaughnessy struck a match and held it to the end of the cigar. The smoke was blue and followed the heat from the gas fire through the fishing nets that decorated the ceiling. "What more can I tell you? She dabbled successfully in finance, unsuccessfully in men. It was as though she had seized on them as her special penance, a way of expiating the sin of having been born Leona O'Brugha, Ireland's most recent Queen Etain. And the more reprehensible or weird the man, the better she liked him."

"How did you, her father, feel about all this—philandering?" O'Shaughnessy asked. The Garda superintendent was very conservative in matters of morals and religion.

"For shame, my Galway friend. I recognize your accent. Keep ever mindful of the fact that strict monogamy was an imposition of two alien cultures—one Christian, the other what is now known as British—on our ancient civilization, in which one's sexual activity and preferences were mostly one's own business."

"But Ovens?" McGarr asked. "Did she consent—"

"That was a political decision which I made. The

cargo he brought in last trip disturbed him. He didn't completely understand the situation here and told us he was through. Leona paid for the repair of his vessel, which, mind you, he had damaged in our service. Inexplicably, that set him off. If he couldn't take care of the boat himself, it didn't seem to be any good to him anymore. He told me it just pointed out to him what the *Virelay* and he had done. He read every Dublin paper looking for deaths, maimings, and injuries caused by the bombs or rockets in the North and agonized over every one of them. He felt that he and that boat were the authors of every little tragedy in the Six Counties.

"And he just loafed around the yacht club come-day-go-day, debating, it seemed to me—I mean, could there be any other explanation for those eternal fits of despondency?—whether or not he'd blow the whistle on us. Even if, as you now tell me, he'd probably never have done that, his being there with that battered boat, the gun oil in his crankcase, would cause somebody, like you two, to ask questions. I have spent far too many years in prison to have to end my days there or in exile. That's what this peripatetic tippling is for me, you see—the actuation of the idea, which is sometimes hard for me to believe, that Mairtín O'Brugha is free, not some semihuman slug ensconced in a lightless cell with only a blanket, no clothes for cover, and the guards wearing rubber-soled shoes so as not to disturb the solitude of my reflections. During the day they even took away the blanket." He finished his drink. "Does that settle your questions?" He stood. "Shall we go?"

"One more," said McGarr. "Does Ovens know who you are?"

"Of course, which is the reason he didn't talk, although it could be he was too drunk to remember the accident at all. I made sure he was stinko. My cause is not cruelty."

As they made for the door, O'Shaughnessy asked, "Can Ovens speak?"

"Yes."

"But does he?"

"Leona once told me he chooses not to speak, since, unlike other men, he realizes there is nothing to say. This makes him very wise in her opinion. Now, how he could have communicated his wisdom to her is a mystery to me."

"He has a certain look about him," said O'Shaughnessy.

" 'That certain carriage of the body which masks the deficiencies of the brain,' said the Irishman when speaking of gravity." O'Brugha fitted on his cloth cap.

McGarr stopped at the door and asked him, "Aren't you going to pick up your change?"

"What for? I'll be back. He'll credit my account."

O'Shaughnessy corrected the old man. "Better to think of it this way—where you're going you won't be needing the cash."

7

And all the way back to Dublin, some twelve miles, McGarr wrestled with the dilemma of whether Mairtín O'Brugha would indeed keep the freedom that allowed him his diurnal round of peripatetic tippling, or whether McGarr would put him back in prison, an action that was almost sure to put McGarr himself out of the chief inspectorship of the Dublin Castle Garda and perhaps into prison with the ancient revolutionary.

McGarr had always prided himself on being a model policeman. He did not act strictly by the rule book, but he did scrupulously avoid confusing his own self-interest with the job. And here, the situation was clear-cut. He must either quash the case, which he could do by asking Ovens if O'Brugha had clubbed him and, when the silent Yank refused to answer, McGarr could say they lacked proof to prosecute; or he must send the evidence they had (including the old man's confession, verbal though it was) to the courts and, same day no doubt, find himself charged with the theft of that report.

One thing was certain, however. Noreen had been right about McGarr's feelings for his new job. He had spent far too long as an exile in other people's countries, enforcing other people's laws, and waiting for the right vacancy back home. It was still a thrill for him to wake up in the morning and realize he was not in Lisbon or Haifa or Leghorn but Rathmines, County Dublin. McGarr was not young, and because he had been honest, he was not rich. He had no children. But could he even think he had a career if he truckled to Horrigan?

McGarr's thoughts ceased with finality when the Rover bounced over the gate jamb and swung into the cobblestone courtyard of the Castle.

There, surrounding his Cooper, was a group of policemen, most of them from Internal Security. Will Hare had opened the Cooper's small trunk. Glumly he looked at McGarr and shook his head.

McGarr and O'Shaughnessy got out of the car and walked through the crowd. The policemen pushed back to let them pass through their cordon of blue chests.

McGarr said, "Don't tell me: something stinks here." He had just remembered the whiting he had gotten from the gardener in Killiney on Saturday morning. He added, "An anonymous phone call to boot."

"In Irish," said Hare.

McGarr turned and looked into the Rover at O'Brugha, who winked.

The trunk also contained the Bombing Report.

"Man's voice or woman's?" McGarr asked. O'Brugha hadn't had a chance to call Hare.

"Woman's."

Neila Monahan, McGarr thought. Twice he had wondered why Horrigan, who must be a very busy man, would have chosen such an old secretary, a woman who was past seventy, whose family had been so closely associated with elements that the present government eschewed. "Old, quavering?"

"A voice," Hare shrugged. He plainly disliked the position the trunkload of documents put him in—having to pass judgment on the country's premier detective and his good friend, whom he would have to interrogate, about whom he would have to submit a report, perhaps even asking for charges to be pressed. "But, now that you mention it, the voice *was* old. This looks bad, Peter. The paper came from Castle supplies. We've checked on it."

"Fingerprints?"

"We're going over that now."

"I'll be in my office."

Walking toward the stairs, McGarr asked O'Brugha, "How many times have you been here?"

"I don't know. Dozens. I can't remember. Are you going to go through with it?"

"I am," said McGarr.

O'Shaughnessy reached over and clapped McGarr on the back.

"Then I suspect it'll be my last. If I were the sentimental sort, I'd take a final look around as though the place meant something to me."

McGarr liked this old man. Here, as both of them were walking into unpleasant situations from which neither of them might ever extract himself, the old boy was joking. He had gone this road before.

After O'Shaughnessy had handed O'Brugha over to Dick Delaney for processing, he said to McGarr,

"Don't worry about this, Peter. The boys"—he tilted his head toward the staff in the office—"and me will eventually prove Horrigan himself stole that report. It's only a matter of time. He's got to have slipped up somewhere."

"Well, maybe he has already. Let's talk, Liam." McGarr walked through the office and gestured to Bernie McKeon and Hughie Ward. They joined them in McGarr's cubicle.

McGarr took off his hat and coat and lit up a Woodbine. Down on the quay, a red setter was coursing along the tree belt, chasing the squirrels that had been browsing the litter on the sidewalk. On his desk was O'Brugha's official dossier. He opened it and scanned several pages. The other men respected his silence. Finally, he said, "Fact: Ovens sustained injuries to his head that could in no way be self-inflicted and most probably were not accidental. Fact: O'Brugha was one of three persons close to Ovens when the injuries occurred. Fact: O'Brugha's fingerprints are on the winch handle. Fact: he has confessed."

"Bingo!" said Bernie McKeon. "Crime solved, chief inspector sacked."

Said McGarr, "That's what bothers me"—he smiled slightly—"apart from the chief inspector getting sacked and all—why the quick confession? If Special Branch couldn't get anything out of O'Brugha in fifteen years, why was he so willing to confess to us? Otherwise, we only have his fingerprints and our supposition that he was the only person near enough to bash Ovens' sconce. Then why would O'Brugha, who has had vast experience in assassinations and executions, have chosen that occasion to conk Ovens and that weapon, the winch handle? He has given us a plausible explanation, but I remain unconvinced. Surely he would have used his gun. And what bothers me most is why David Horrigan would risk his whole political career to cover up the final crime of an aged recidivist."

"Without that confession," said O'Shaughnessy, "we wouldn't have a thing. He was chummy with Ovens, and they drank together. There's no reason why his fingerprints shouldn't be on that winch handle. A tax attorney could get the case thrown out of court."

"It's the woman," said Hughie Ward. "She's the key to the whole thing."

They all turned to him.

Bernie McKeon began jibing. "Would you listen to our young Lothario. He's got women on the brain."

"She's got to be," Ward insisted. "I'm not saying this because I think she's—" He flushed.

"Beautiful," McGarr supplied. "Because she is." He turned to his men. "Are we agreed?"

They all nodded.

"It's because she's—different from your usual beautiful woman. She's got something else."

"She's rich," said McKeon.

"No—not just that. She's—" Ward groped for the right word but couldn't find it.

All of them, however, knew what he had meant. She was different, entirely.

McGarr said, "Why don't we talk to her some more, then." He checked his wristwatch. It was half past eleven. "Send out for some sandwiches and tea, Bernie."

"Tea?" McKeon questioned. "You'll have me running to the jakes at fifteen-minute intervals and most probably at the point when I'm about to exonerate you in toto."

"All right—a dozen bottles of lager."

"Two dozen," said McKeon.

"A dozen and a half." McGarr turned to the window. A fine rain was blurring the glass.

Just one day in jail seemed to have taken a toll on Leona Horrigan. In the direct beam of the shaded light, her face seemed gaunt, her cheeks just slightly hollow, her green eyes shadowed by the sweep of her eyebrows, recessed, older. Still, her figure was full and angular in a green cashmere sweater and black skirt, her posture erect on the bentwood chair. Now and again, she pushed her long black hair from in front of her eyes.

For two hours Liam O'Shaughnessy went over her signed statement concerning her activities on the afternoon of the attack upon Ovens. She was again asked about the blood-spattered shoes and dress, her relationship with Ovens, why she had paid his yard bill, who her contacts in the IRA were, how much money she spent on the guns, bombs, and her other illegal activities.

Through it all, she spoke seldom, answered only those questions that were in no way incriminating, and seemed bored by the entire process.

When Bernie McKeon took over, he tried a new tack. In a soft voice he began reading from her father's dossier, "O'Brugha, Mairtín. Born third December, 1902, at Clifden, County Galway." McKeon broke off. He was sitting close enough to share the light with her. "Now—why did I think that poor old man was from Cork?" His puffy face seemed innocent, trusting, familiar.

McGarr was standing in the shadows near the door to his office. Dick Delaney was taking the log of the interrogation in the far corner of the room.

McKeon said, "Ah—now I know." He lifted several pages of the dossier. "Married Megan Moriarty of Cobh, twenty-second June, 1931. Child: Leona Honora Margaret-Mary—that's you—O'Brugha, born sixteenth July, 1933, Cork City, and a fine piece of work, if you don't mind my saying so myself, Leona. May I call you that?"

She only drew on the cigarette.

"Now then," McKeon turned back to page one. "A precocious child, this Mairtín O'Brugha. Heralded all the way up. Here is a copy of his performance in school. In the margin, the schoolmaster has written this accolade." McKeon glanced over at her, his eyes smiling and playful. "We'll see how good Leitrim Gaelic is. 'A mind quicker than a' something or other, 'and as deep as—' " He craned his head to McGarr, "Can you make this out, Peter? The schoolmaster in my town was my granduncle. I passed on a special dispensation."

"Light," she said in a tired voice. "The flux of time."

"Oh—oh, yes." McKeon again looked at her playfully. "Gaelic is given to exaggeration, isn't it?"

Her eyes flashed at him.

McKeon had succeeded in getting an emotional reaction from her and began building on it. "But how do you know so much about your father? Wasn't he always 'away,' so to speak?"

"Precisely," she hissed. "That's all I really had to know—his criminal file."

"And such a pity it is to read too, such a waste. First honors in his Leaving Certificate. A stipend, a grant, later a moderatorship at University College. Again First Class honors but this time with Special Distinction in both ancient and modern languages, and here we have"—he turned a page—"a copy of a letter from a don at Cambridge saying all expenses will be met, lodging arranged, and a small stipend provided. That's 1927.

"But he wouldn't take the King's shilling, would he? No. The Sorbonne—studied Greek, Latin, Hebrew, and Gaelic. Then on to European travels. Now, let's see—where was your mother all this time, back home in Ireland pining for her wandering scholar?" McKeon searched through the dossier.

Hughie Ward tapped McGarr on the shoulder, and when the chief turned to him, he motioned McGarr into the office. Ward shut the door and they walked into McGarr's cubicle. Ward pointed to the phone. "It's Sinclair. He's found Driver."

"Really?" McGarr was very pleased. "He's good, that Sinclair." He reached for the phone. "Paul? Where are you?"

"O'Donahue's on St. Stephen's Green, the sing-song pub where all the musicians and tourists congregate. Driver has been here all along. The barman said he slept here last night. From his personal effects, all I can deduce is that he probably went straight to the Shelbourne and got paid off by Horrigan, nipped into Barclay's Bank to stash the best part of the funds in his pass-book account, which I've got in my hands now, and then made a tour of the pubs around the Green. He only got this far before he succumbed."

"Not dead, I hope."

"Not actually. I've called an ambulance. A German doctor here, a tourist, says he should have his stomach pumped, should be put on intravenous feeding and dried out. Doesn't look as though he has eaten in weeks."

"We'll have a patrol accompany him to the hospital"

—McGarr signaled to Ward, who began copying down the orders—"and a man stationed by his bedside. No visitors. I want somebody to take down everything he says. Hughie will be over at the St. Stephen's Green branch of Barclay's Bank in a half hour with a writ to examine Driver's transactions. That is his branch, isn't it, Paul?"

"Yes. He only lives—er, used to live right around the corner."

"I want you to do that just in case Horrigan slipped up and paid him off by check." McGarr thought for a moment. "Oh, my God."

"What's wrong, Chief?"

"What was the amount of the deposit?"

"You're not going to believe this. It was ten thousand pounds. How stupid can Horrigan be? Driver has probably told half of Dublin about the money by now."

Sinclair could not have known that three days before, in Naas, Horrigan had handed McGarr a cashier's check, which McGarr had grasped, then let go. "In this case, Paul, Driver's alcoholism is working in Horrigan's favor. Say, for instance, we can get Driver to change his story to the truth. Horrigan will say it's the booze talking and then mention our official record that contains proof of Driver's whereabouts on the night of the supposed theft.

"Also," McGarr added, "we'd better get the Technical Bureau to do a complete fingerprint analysis on the cashier's check."

"How do you know it's a cashier's check?"

"Trust me." McGarr opened the top drawer of his desk and shut it again. "I know. But maybe we can discover a Horrigan latent. We'll have Hughie see if he can trace the source of the funds as well. I know what we're going to find, however."

"You do?"

"McGarr's fingerprints on the check, McGarr's description from the bank teller who made it out. Horrigan probably scoured the thirty-two counties for a dead ringer for me, then treated the innocent man to a tan raincoat, dark suit, and a derby.

"Hughie will meet you at the bank, Paul. Good work." McGarr hung up.

Now, more than ever, McGarr needed Leona Horrigan's confession. He walked through the office and opened the door to the day room.

McKeon was still talking to her in the same soft tone. "Two years in Bologna, it says here, but it doesn't say why he went there or what he was doing in Italy. Could he have turned to honest labor at last?"

"His health," she supplied. "He had developed a cough in Paris. How he got on is nobody's business, since, it seems, he survived."

"That—that he did. Lived four years and seven months in Florence. I wonder how he got on there."

"Tutored while he studied history at the university."

"He also became involved with the establishment of the Italian Communist Party—sounds bad, doesn't it? I hear you're a capitalist of no slight leverage yourself, ma'am."

"He's entitled to his beliefs. I'm not a capitalist, I'm a realist."

"It seems you must have gotten all that practicality from your mother, since from the time of your father's leaving Florence in the late twenties right up until today—we've got him downstairs, you know; he's confessed to the attempted murder of Ovens; they'll put him away for good this time—his career as a human being has been all downhill. Murder, assassinations, bank robberies, gunrunning, sabotage, kidnapping, espionage for a hostile foreign power. No sooner was he released from prison than he was involved in some dirty deed or another, and there he was again, back in the pokey. One death sentence was commuted because the Taoseaich respected his mind, another because he had information concerning the IRA hierarchy, which David Nelligan believed they could pull out of him down at the Curragh.

"Well, this time it's no noble cause, is it?" McKeon placed the dossier on his lap and folded his arms across his chest. "It's just a bloody ugly little deed—trying to take the life of an unworldly, quiet, kindly man whose only crime was to love you, Leona, and hate the part he played in running antipersonnel weaponry into the North at your insistence."

McGarr thought he saw her wince a little when McKeon alluded to Ovens, but she said, "Cheap histrionics again, Sergeant? Please try to moderate your technique. Even the most convincing dramatic performance grows stale after a time."

McKeon suddenly bawled, "Well, why do *you* think an experienced Fenian would ever even consider trying to conk a man with a winch handle in broad daylight? Do you think he would botch the job? Why does the man who resisted all the atrocities of the Curragh confess in five minutes? Why does he come along with us meek as a lamb? Because he feels his life is over, because he doesn't want his only sibling to rot in the can the way he did? Things don't match up here, and I'm betting you're such a cold bitch you can sit there and watch him do it! I bet you're such a 'realist' you can clap him into a cell for the rest of his life and not even bat an eye."

She looked over at McGarr in the shadows, smirked, and drew deeply on the cigarette. Her skin, which was very white, was just slightly translucent and reminded McGarr of Carrara marble that had been smoothed to a gloss. She said, "My father is nothing but a jailbird anyhow. Have you ever thought of that? Maybe he'd never admit it, but it's what he has always wanted, what he got for most of his life, and what he deserves."

That was when McGarr pushed himself off the wall. "I don't believe you mean that. Get O'Brugha up here, Bernie. We'll let her tell that to his face." McGarr had dealt with people like Leona Horrigan before. As long as she could dehumanize her conception of her father, she could make him her scapegoat. McGarr wondered if her father had ever told her about his fifteen years—a record, the dossier stated—in the Curragh solitary cells. McGarr doubted it. O'Brugha was a hard man, just the sort who would keep the ugliness of his imprisonment from his family at all costs.

And the old man was haggard. McKeon had awakened him and he looked as though he had aged ten years since McGarr had first seen him on the Killiney Yacht Club docks four days before. His jawbone protruded right back to his ears. His eyes were glazed and he breathed through his mouth. His hand shook when McGarr gave him a bottle of Harp.

His daughter hadn't looked up when he entered the room.

McGarr didn't offer O'Brugha a chair, just stood him across the table from his daughter.

After taking a swig of beer, the old man cleared his throat and, placing the bottle on the table, rubbed his eyes. The room was utterly silent. O'Brugha's narrow shoulders barely held his suspenders. "How are you keeping, Leona? Have they been hard on you? Where's your solicitor? You ought to have one, you know. Hadn't she?" he asked McGarr.

Still she hadn't as much as glanced at her father.

McGarr said, "We haven't yet used the cattle prods on her, Mairtín. After that, if she has told us what we want to know, she can call her solicitor."

O'Brugha jerked his neck toward McGarr. He tried to smile. He realized McGarr was codding him, but it was as though the prison atmosphere of the Castle had reminded the old man of other days and other practices. "You boys don't do that sort of thing any—" He glanced down at his daughter.

"No, we don't. But they did it to you, didn't they, Mairtín—out in the Curragh? Haven't you told Leona about your fifteen years of solitary in a tiny iron cell no bigger than a steamer trunk? No heat, no light but what little came through the slit. How about the guards, Mairtín? Tell Leona what you told us out at the Harbour Bar about the Curragh. What sort of shoes did the guards wear?"

O'Brugha's light blue eyes flashed down on his daughter's head, then back to McGarr. He knew what McGarr had in mind, how these questions would work on Leona's pity for him.

"What kind were they, Liam?" McGarr asked O'Shaughnessy. "Can you remember what he said they were?"

"Rubber shoes—'so as not to disturb the solitude of one's reflections' was the way he put it."

"And how long like that? Certainly fifteen years is a"—McGarr searched for the right word—"hyperbole."

Leona Horrigan had raised her head and was staring at her father.

His eyes were moving about the shadows, seeing anything, everything but his daughter's face, upon which the lamp over the day-room table shone brightest.

"Surely there must have been a break, a month, a day, several hours, a week at least?"

O'Shaughnessy answered McGarr. "Every prison has an exercise yard, Peter."

O'Brugha was swaying beside the table. He put out his hand and steadied himself. When he looked up, his eyes met his daughter's. "It doesn't matter," he said. "Sure and I could do a thousand years standing on my head. They're just trying to box you in, Leona. Don't be taken in by him." O'Brugha pointed to McGarr. "He's worse than any of them. He's Nelligan but with greater guile. My life is over. When all is said and done, I rather like prison. Nowadays, they let you have books, a little job, the food isn't half bad, and—"

"How long were the exercise periods?" she asked.

"Oh"—he flicked a hand off the tabletop—"hours—three, four."

"Five minutes," said McGarr, "including the time it took them to haul you to and from your cell. How many times did they chuck you into that treeless courtyard, O'Brugha, and you too stiff to crawl through the clinkers? And nude! The IRA wouldn't recognize the Free State, Leona—you know this, don't you?—and so the prisoners refused to wear prison uniforms. You got a thin army blanket at night, but they took that away in the morning, didn't they, Mairtín?"

O'Shaughnessy asked, "And how many years all told did you spend in prison? Twenty? Thirty years? Not *thirty* years!"

"Thirty-four years," said Leona Horrigan and lowered her head.

"Time is relative," O'Brugha said, sensing that they had broken her resolve. In his own way, he was pleading with her to keep her peace. "The years just flew by. I was there, now I'm here. Simple as that. It wasn't at all as tough as they make out. A man has time for reflection, contemplation, meditation, just like the saints of old."

McGarr asked, "And how about visions. Did you have any of those, Mairtín?"

Forgetting himself, O'Brugha said, "Oh yes—a man can find a great depth of solace in the *proper* vision."

Again she looked up at him.

"You place such emphasis on the word 'proper,' " said McKeon.

"A word that is in vogue today is 'hallucination,' " said McGarr.

"And did you talk to yourself too, Mairtín?" asked O'Shaughnessy.

Leona Horrigan slowly turned just her head to McGarr. She was about to say something, when O'Brugha's hand jumped across the table and grasped his daughter's, which were folded in front of her. "Don't, Leona. You can still take it back. Your solicitor isn't present. They didn't inform you of your rights. I'm an old man. A few more years wouldn't touch me."

She stared down at their hands. Her eyes were blinking rapidly. It was as though she were trying to summon either the courage to confess or the heartlessness to continue with the ruse that her father had committed the crime and would take her punishment for her.

McGarr said to Delaney, "Read her last statement before we brought O'Brugha up here, Dick."

But before Delaney could flip through his notes, she said, "You're nothing but a jailbird anyhow, Mairtín. Maybe you've never admitted it to yourself, but it's what you've always wanted and what you deserve."

The old man's thin face received the words like blows. He staggered slightly and said, "Ah, yes. Yes."

McGarr carried a chair over to the table and placed it alongside Leona's. He then helped O'Brugha into it. The old man kept patting her hands until she withdrew them.

Out in the office, McGarr said to Liam O'Shaughnessy, "I can't sit around here and wait for her to crack."

"She's a hard case. You'd be older than O'Brugha before that happened."

"So it's time for us to be as devious as Horrigan, Liam. Have Slattery type up a report of this case. Use the interrogation log right up until that last bit where she denied him a second time. Then put in something like, 'I tried to murder Bobby Ovens because he told me everything he ever had to do with me was foul—the guns, the bombs, my money, everything, including the way I paid his boatyard bill without asking him. And he was so damnably professional in his innocence, so American and officiously upright.' That should do it. That's what she wanted to say.

"Then take the report over to the Taoseaich's office. Tell his secretary you want to make an appointment for me for"—McGarr checked his wristwatch; it was 2:10 in the afternoon—"say four-thirty. Leave nothing out about the Bombing Report or anything else. Then wait for me there." McGarr turned as though he would walk away. "Oh"—he turned back—"one other thing. Please make sure you don't leave the office for any reason. When that phone call comes, you've got to be there."

O'Shaughnessy didn't understand and was worried. "Just the one false note?" He'd have to sign the report himself.

"Don't worry, Liam. I'll say I misinformed you on purpose, if it comes to that."

O'Shaughnessy was only somewhat relieved. Dishonesty of any sort bothered him terribly. "Where are you going?"

"Has Hubbard been released?"

"He got himself a solicitor—we had to let him go."

McGarr could see Ward and Sinclair waiting for him in his cubicle. "Then I'm off to play poker."

O'Shaughnessy looked down at McGarr in astonishment. "Not at a time like—" He was a gullible man for all his police experience.

"Two hands only. One with Hubbard and the other with Horrigan. They've got all the cards and I've got no choice but to try to bluff my way through." McGarr didn't add that the stakes he was gambling with were his reputation, career, and spotless criminal record. If he lost he'd have to buy a farm with his small savings and work it, because nobody would hire him after being sacked and jailed for high treason.

In his cubicle Ward said, "It's like you guessed, chief. Your fingerprints are on that check." Ward looked at McGarr as though he wanted him to give a plausible explanation.

"Any latents?"

"No, just several good impressions of Driver's."

"What about him, Paul?"

"Well, when I gave him a complete search at the hospital, I found this in his back pocket. He was sitting on it all the time we were at O'Donahue's." Sinclair handed McGarr a legal-size sheet of paper that had at one time been folded down to a three-inch square.

It was a confession, stating that Driver had delivered the Bombing Report to McGarr in two parts, one on the night of the twenty-third of October, 1975, at the Royal Hotel in Glendalough, and the second on the morning of the twenty-fifth at the Dolphin in Dun Laoghaire. There McGarr had paid him ten thousand pounds in the form of a cashier's check.

"May I have a photocopy of these?" If McGarr was going to play poker, he at least needed a hand, even if all his cards were valueless.

While Hughie ran the documents through the machine, McGarr put on his hat and coat, then asked McKeon to accompany him. "Make sure you have a fresh pad, Bernie. I'm going to ask you to take a statement that I hope we can get signed."

Next, they stopped at Will Hare's Internal Security office. Will himself came out of his cubicle to greet them. "Going somewhere?" he asked. He was worried. "Things look mighty bad, Peter. Awful."

"Talk to Ward and Sinclair and they'll look worse," said McGarr. "Look, Will—you wouldn't just happen to have a copy of that Bombing Report hanging about that I could borrow, would you?"

"You must be mad. Is he right?" Hare asked McKeon.

"Not the real thing, just, say, the cover, the introduction, and then a number of filler pages so that it looks thick and important."

Hare began shaking his head. He was a thin man with a beard so heavy and a face so creased he could not manage to shave properly. Thus he always looked rough and countryish. "I can't do that, Peter. I've got to answer for those things. It's impossible."

"Even if, in so doing, you might clear up the whole messy business?"

"How?"

McKeon turned to McGarr as well. He too was interested in knowing what McGarr had in mind.

"Trust me."

"That I can't do."

"Where's the stuff?"

Hare's eyes jerked involuntarily toward a walk-in safe at the back of the Internal Security office. The door was open.

McGarr started for it.

"Well—Jesus, Mary, and Joseph," said Hare. "Stay out of there, Peter. Stop. You don't have a security clearance." He ran after McGarr.

"I don't want the report, I just want a dummy. Something that looks like it."

"Je-sus! You'll get me fired. Aren't you in enough trouble already?"

Now inside the vault, McGarr found the Bombing Report among a stack of most-secret documents. "Now watch." He picked up the black leather notebook and consulted the index. The report was thick, over a thousand pages, and listed every detail of every injury, damage suit, police lead, and allegation uncovered in a two-and-one-half-month investigation.

McGarr slapped it down on a carton, unclasped its

binder, and removed all but the forty-seven-page introduction. He then reached onto another shelf containing less secret information and pulled out an equally thick volume that was called "Postal Authority Maintenance Concerns in Nineteenth-Century Structures." McGarr removed the pages and carefully fitted those into the Bombing Report binder. "There now, does that satisfy you?" he asked Hare. He turned and started out of the vault.

"No! No, it doesn't at all. I'll have to report you. I should try to stop you."

McGarr turned to Hare. "I'll have it back by sundown. That's a promise."

Hare sighed. "All right—sundown. I'll be waiting."

It was the first time that McGarr had ever seen McKeon at a loss for words.

8

The ceiling of McDaid's pub was sheathed in ornate tin and painted, like the walls, a glossy cream color. Tall, arched windows made it perhaps the brightest barroom in the country. The bar itself was small. Men three deep were standing by it, reaching for the glasses that they kept on its top. The atmosphere was thick with smoke, voices, and the cheers of the hurling crowd on the television.

Hubbard was sitting alone with his back to the screen.

Seeing McGarr, the barman picked a newspaper off the counter behind him, opened it to an inside page, and showed it to several men with whom he had been talking. It was a picture of McGarr and O'Shaughnessy walking O'Brugha into the Castle. The caption read: "Chief Inspector McGarr solves another crime that might have gone unnoticed, story, page 11." How much of what is printed in the newspapers, McGarr mused, is the whole truth? "Not a bad likeness, what?" he asked the barman, who was mixing a gin and tonic for Hubbard. The drinks were on the house.

McGarr touched the brim of his hat to thank the man, and McKeon carried the glasses over to Hubbard's table.

McGarr was very weary now. When he sat and removed his derby, he realized that most conversation in the tavern had ceased. How small his country was, the people as gossipy here in Dublin as in any small town in the West.

Hubbard had drained his glass and now began drinking from the one McGarr had brought him. The fat young man was drunk, his face puffy, eyes red-rimmed. Several shreds of tobacco from the pipe he was smoking had snagged in his beard.

McGarr said, "She has confessed."

Hubbard only shook his head, then sipped from the glass.

"She said, 'I tried to kill Bobby Ovens because he told me everything he ever had to do with me was foul—the guns, the bombs, my money, everything, including the way I paid his boatyard bill without asking him. And he was so damnably professional in his innocence, so American and so officiously upright.' " McGarr had said the statement offhandedly, as if it were a fact and rather uninteresting. Little could Hubbard have known how important the ploy was to McGarr.

Hubbard lowered the glass and stared into it. He held it in both hands. "Well," he said after some time, "It's true that Ovens was the only man who ever abandoned her. After he found out what the cargo really contained, after she tried to meddle in the relationship Ovens has with that boat of his, he cut her off. She couldn't stand it. She focused all her hatred for—" Hubbard raised the glass and said "men" into it, drank the liquor, and then added, "on him." Hubbard set the nearly empty glass down. "Does this mean you're here to arrest me?"

"Yes. We'll arrest Ovens too. Both of you conspired with Leona Horrigan to conceal evidence. And both of you joined David Horrigan in an attempt to falsify the theft of most-secret government documents and to propagate a conspiracy involving charges of high treason, the attempted calumny of a public official—namely me—and blackmail." McGarr, picking the copy of the Bombing Report off the floor and slapping it down on the table, added, "Here's the high treason."

Hubbard picked up the binder and turned to the title page, which had MOST SECRET stamped across it in red.

"And here"—McGarr slapped the photocopy of the ten-thousand-pound check and the other one of Driver's confession in front of Hubbard—"is the calumny of a public official and the blackmail."

Hubbard picked up the check and stared blankly at the ten-thousand-pound figure. He then glanced through Driver's confession. After he put it down, he said, "Oh no—there you are very wrong, McGarr. That's not me, and certainly not Ovens. I had nothing to do with that piece of oak tag you found in my study nor any of this stuff here. That sounds like Horrigan. We—and by that I mean Leona and Ovens too; the man, no matter how repugnant, has character—we would never attack a person for the simple reason of personal expediency." He was shaking his head. "No—that's not us."

"Why did she hit him?"

"Who knows?" Hubbard was looking toward the barman, who was watching the television.

McKeon had his pen poised on a sheet of his pad.

"They had their usual spat on the dock. It was as you said, but he was dirty drunk and didn't even wait for her to start beating him." Again Hubbard craned his neck toward the barman. "You know, ever since he delivered that shipment of arms, which was, when all was said and done, more of a token gesture—given the diminutive size of his boat—than an important contribution to our needs in the North, he's been an unmitigated ass. But she didn't seem to want to let him go. She kept plaguing him, buying him things, paying his bills, slipping money in his wallet. All he did was drink. The more he drank the more he withdrew into himself. And that just made her more desperate to get a rise out of him."

McGarr signaled for another round, then said, "She's a big, powerful woman. Why didn't the blows kill Ovens?"

"We all—O'Brugha, Leona, and I—had our hands on the winch handle. No matter how much Ovens might have discomfited us—me because of Leona, O'Brugha because of Ovens' curious behavior—neither of us would have consented to killing him. After his own fashion, Ovens is something of a gentleman. He has his own odd sort of—style. And he certainly is not untalented."

"You mean, she just grabbed the handle on impulse and bashed him?"

Hubbard looked up from the fresh drink, which McGarr had just paid for with a crisp five-pound note. "I thought you said she confessed."

McGarr nodded. "But I lied. I only said it for the effect, which I'm enjoying thoroughly." He took a sip from the porter.

Hubbard raised the fresh gin and tonic to his lips

and drained it right down. "Horse show," he said in a voice that the liquor made high. "She had just come from the one in Ballsbridge. She had gloves on."

"Ovens didn't fall in the water right off. How'd that happen?"

"Does this all come under the heading of cooperation?"

McGarr shrugged, "That's for the prosecutor to decide, but I'll be sure to tell him."

"Well, we didn't push him in, let me assure you. After he went down on the deck, he lay there for a time. Meanwhile, I went to call an ambulance and Mairtín went for a first-aid kit and a litter. We hadn't gotten halfway down the dock when he suddenly scrambled to his feet, fell once more, got up, and tripped over the hatch to his ice chest. He fell into the slip. The moment Mairtín got the boat hook on him, the bloody horn went off on the hill. If it hadn't been for that horn—"

McGarr stared into the amber head of the stout in the pint glass, watching the rainbow surfaces of the bubbles burst. "I can understand why O'Brugha wanted to cover up this thing—he didn't want to see his daughter go to prison. In part, I can understand why Horrigan went to such lengths—she is his wife, her IRA involvement would damage his chances to become Taoseaich in the near future, and he saw an opportunity to compromise the independence of the Garda and name his own successor to me. Ovens himself well may have had many reasons for not saying anything—he was drunk and doesn't remember, the trauma eradicated his memory of the event, or the whole thing was only an argument that snowballed and he prefers now to forget it. But you, Hubbard, stump me. Other than her being an extraordinarily beautiful woman, what were your reasons for going along with the cover-up?"

Hubbard reached over and picked up McGarr's second pint of stout. The chief inspector hadn't touched it. Hubbard raised it in a salute, then drank down half. The foam clung to his moustache, making his lips seem very red. "I don't know, to be honest. Let's leave it at that."

Both McGarr and McKeon looked up at him.

Hubbard smiled. "That she's an extraordinarily beautiful woman. As Eochu said when he first saw Etain, 'I would leave all the world's women for her sake.' "

"Consider it done," said McKeon.

"What time would you like to report to my office in the Castle tomorrow?" McGarr didn't want to disturb Hubbard in his present state. He had gotten from him what he wanted. Certainly, the fat young man wouldn't get very far in his present condition.

"What time do you suggest?"

"Whenever it's convenient to you."

"That's very good of you, old man."

"It's the least I can do for you. In time you'll realize how important this conversation was to my career." McGarr stood.

McKeon slid the pad toward Hubbard and handed him his pen.

"Do I have to?"

"It's the truth, isn't it?" McKeon demanded.

Hubbard nodded.

"Then what are you afraid of?"

Hubbard signed the pad. Tomorrow, after McKeon had typed up a formal statement, Hubbard would be asked to sign that as well. "It's just what you okayed last night, sir. If it was the truth then, it's got to be the truth now," McKeon would say. That way the question of the drinks and McGarr's little lie could be avoided in court.

McKeon flipped the pad shut, retrieved his pen, and stood.

"Where are you going?" Hubbard asked them.

"To speak to Horrigan and then to Ovens."

Hubbard snorted drunkenly into the pint glass. "And good luck to you, Inspector."

On the way to the door, McGarr called the Taoseaich's office to add Hubbard's admissions to the report of the Ovens attack investigation. O'Shaughnessy was there.

McGarr dropped Bernie McKeon and the dummy Bombing Report off at the Castle and turned back toward St. Stephen's Green and the Shelbourne Hotel. In the poker hand he was about to play with Horrigan, he needed no other cards than the information Hubbard had just given him and Liam O'Shaughnessy's presence in the Taoseaich's office.

It had stopped raining and a brisk wind was driving the storm clouds from the sky. Every so often the sun broke through and cast a pale light on the narrow streets and faded brick buildings of Georgian Dublin.

McGarr noted that the trees on the Green had already turned, and, as he parked his car across from the Shelbourne, a leaf storm swirled over the walk and eddied in the quiet air by the side of the Cooper.

This afternoon the Shelbourne did not seem the comfortable city abode of the Irish Ascendancy that McGarr had always thought it. This afternoon the hotel was dark, too hot, its hallways timeworn and cramped.

He knocked on the door of Horrigan's suite, then turned the knob.

David Horrigan was sitting at a towering escritoire, the shelves and nooks of which were crammed with papers. It was obviously an antique, many of the perpendiculars warped with age. Several long tables were covered with files. Horrigan obviously did much of his work here. He had his back to McGarr and was bent over a pad, on which he was writing with great speed. "Peter? I've been expecting you. Is this going to be our showdown? If so, here's my case." He ripped the sheet off his pad and handed it to McGarr. It read:

Alleged: that Peter McGarr was involved in the theft of the Bombing Report. That on two occasions the Report was passed by Carleton Driver, the confessed thief, to McGarr: 1) the Royal Hotel, Glendalough, the night of 23rd October, 1975; 2) the Dolphin Lounge Bar or Dalton's Turf Accountant's shop on the morning of 25th October, 1975. That McGarr was found to be in possession of the stolen Report which was discovered in the trunk of his automobile in the courtyard of Dublin Castle 28th October, 1975. That McGarr paid £10,000 to Carleton Driver for the receipt of the Report.

Proof: Garda file 37204–A.

"As you can see, I plan to use your own file against you. You're a good policeman and you've built a solid case against yourself."

"What's my motive?"

"Patriotism. You are a covert agent of the IRA." Horrigan opened the middle drawer of the writing desk and pushed a button on a portable tape recorder.

McGarr heard his own voice saying, "I support the IRA."

Another voice, Horrigan's, then asked him, "Well, how much, you know, theoretically?"

"Right down the line. Some tactics, of course, I deplore. For instance, the bombing of any target other than military. Cops are paid to take their chances. But as for the violence itself, have they any option?"

Horrigan stopped the machine, removed the cassette, and put another into it. The machine played a recording of the conversation McGarr had had with Spud Murphy about running to ground in Dingle. Murphy's allusion to McGarr's not as yet being in the IRA had been deleted, however.

McGarr was surprised. Since Horrigan had tapped his phone, he probably knew everything about McGarr's investigation but the false confession.

"Didn't think I'd be so thorough, did you?"

"Don't think for a moment that I underestimated you."

"I didn't include your practice of letting many IRA suspects, like Murphy, off lightly, how you didn't arrest Ovens when you learned he was an arms smuggler, the sheet of oak tag which implicates your wife and gives the name of your contact, Muldoon, in the North, to whom you probably rushed a photocopy of the Bombing Report via Murphy in Galway, and the bank teller who will swear that you purchased that cashier's check, which has your fingerprints on it, because I know you realize any good lawyer, like myself, will raise all those issues.

"And what do you have, Chief Inspector?" Horrigan leaned back in his chair. His curly hair seemed greyer now, his fleshy face and bulbous nose were blotched. McGarr knew he had stomach trouble. Having removed his suit coat, Horrigan was plainly fat.

"Your wife has confessed in her father's presence, and he did not deny her statement, which she signed."

"I don't believe you."

"She had just come from the Dublin Horse Show. She had on white gloves, white shoes, and a flower-print dress. She found Ovens on the dock somewhat drunker than usual, staring at *Virelay* as though the vessel were a dying thing to which she had delivered the mortal blow. And, as usual, he ignored her.

"She started in on him. That day he wouldn't even listen to her. He got up, boarded *Virelay,* and went below. When Hubbard and O'Brugha saw her take the handle from the winch and follow Ovens, they immediately went to his aid. As they approached the boat they could hear her berating him, working herself up into a fit. They got into the cabin just in time to grab her arm and diminish the effect of the blows somewhat. Otherwise, Ovens would be dead.

"Ovens blundered up the companionway and fell onto the deck. Hubbard went for the phone to call an ambulance, at the same time leading Leona away from the vessel. O'Brugha ran for a litter and first-aid kit. No sooner had they gotten down on the dock than Ovens scrambled to his feet, fell again, got up, tripped over the hatch to the ice chest, and tumbled into the slip. The moment that O'Brugha got a boat hook on him, Captain Moran, who was watching them through binoculars from his bungalow up on the hill, set off the emergency siren and called the police."

McGarr reached for the telephone on Horrigan's desk. "What's the Taoseaich's phone number?"

Horrigan consulted a circular file on the desk. "834157."

McGarr dialed the number and handed the phone to Horrigan. "Ask for O'Shaughnessy. Have him read the brief of the report, then the confession itself."

After listening for a while, just as McGarr had expected, Horrigan said, "Put the Taoseaich's secretary on, please." He paused for a moment and said, "This is Minister for Justice Horrigan, Gerald. Does Superintendent O'Shaughnessy have an appointment to see the Taoseaich? Four-thirty and with McGarr. I see—thank you." Horrigan's face was now ashen and drawn.

He got up from the desk and moved to a sideboard. There he bent and drew a decanter from below. He poured a very full glass and handed it to McGarr. "How did you do it? I never doubted for a moment Leona's will to survive or that Mairtín would cave in in any way." Horrigan sat at the desk.

McGarr leaned against one of the long tables.

"You didn't have any real proof before that, did you?"

McGarr shook his head. "All the blood-spattered shoes and dress did was to place her at the scene of the crime. We had a photo too, but that's not proof, since it would be impossible to get an exact time on it. And we couldn't arrest either Ovens or Leona for the gun grease on the hull of *Virelay.*"

"And the old man admitted to the crime?" Horrigan asked.

McGarr nodded.

"That was the plan, you know. If you discovered his identity."

"Did she know about the plan?" McGarr drank from the tumbler.

"Is this off the record?"

McGarr shook his head. "Of course not. Nothing is ever off the record with a policeman."

"What does it matter, really?" Horrigan rubbed his knuckles across the stubble on his cheek. "She came to me right after it happened, and we worked it out together. It was the first thing we had done, you know"—he glanced at McGarr—"together in a long time. Years and years. She wanted my help. That meant something, but we really didn't have time enough to plan properly.

"If only that blasted Moran hadn't touched off the horn. The minute the police arrived, however, it was quite another story."

McGarr thought briefly of the afternoon on the dock. If the weather hadn't been so pleasant, he would have let Hughie Ward and Bernie McKeon handle the junket to Bray. The other two, in a rush to establish themselves at the bar of the Khyber Pass, would have reported Ovens' injury as an accident. So much the better that would have been for all parties concerned, he mused.

"When I found out you were on the case, I panicked." Again Horrigan looked up at McGarr. "Your reputation is formidable, Peter, and deservedly so."

McGarr drained the glass. "Do you still love her?"

Horrigan's brow furrowed. "I certainly must. At least it appears I shall have given up a very great deal for her, enough perhaps to call it love?"

There was a question in Horrigan's voice. McGarr did not want to answer it. He pushed himself off the table. "Have you released the Bombing Report to the papers yet?"

"Unfortunately—this morning."

"That's a shame."

"Yes—I hope it doesn't ruin you, Peter, now that there's no advantage in it for me."

"It certainly won't, if you have the decency to tell the Taoseaich the truth. Otherwise, I'm sure that I can get Driver to crack. We'll dry him out and apply pressure. Now that he can't use the money you gave him, he'll come around."

Horrigan raised his eyebrows.

"I'll impound it as evidence. The trial could drag on for years. Driver will never be able to post bond, and he'll come around in jail. He's the sort of person who needs his"—McGarr looked into his glass—"freedom. In return for reduced charges he'll testify against you." McGarr could be sure of none of this. In the meantime, however, things would become very sticky for the chief inspector. From the very pith of his being, McGarr wanted to convince Horrigan that not owning up to the theft of the Bombing Report now would only bring Horrigan further trouble in the future.

McGarr continued. "But I meant that the real shame is your having let the thing go. If you hadn't been so hasty, I was willing to let all your"—McGarr fished for the right word—"peccadilloes drop. After all, we understand each other now."

"You were?" Horrigan reached for the phone. "What if it's still possible?"

McGarr placed the glass on the desk. "Good luck, David." He turned to go.

Horrigan tugged at the sleeve of his raincoat. He took the tape cassettes from the middle drawer of the desk and handed them to McGarr. "No hard feelings?"

"Not now—no."

They shook hands and McGarr left.

In the lobby of the Shelbourne a small boy was ripping the cords off a parcel of *Heralds* that announced the release of the Bombing Report.

9

It was twilight by the time the Cooper crested Dalkey Hill. Setting behind a cloud bank, the sun suffused the western sky with a magenta glow. The Irish Sea was still, save for a fishing boat that was making for Greystones. Its starboard beacon cast a finger of green light on the glassy water. The gentle curve of shoreline from Killiney to Bray Head was dark now.

Even before McGarr geared down the steep hill from the Khyber Pass Hotel, past Captain Moran's white bungalow, and toward the complex of slate roofs, which was the yacht club, he could see the glow of Ovens' cigarette on the dock.

He was seated on the soft-drink case, staring at *Virelay* as she swayed on her dock lines in the wind that now began to blow shoreward with the approach of night. He had a smudge of grease on the bandages that wrapped his head.

McGarr pulled another wooden case off the afterdeck and sat beside Ovens, who handed him a half-empty bottle of rum.

When they had drunk that, Ovens stood. "What's

going to happen to my boat?" he asked. Strangely, his voice was mild, his accent refined.

"Captain Moran and I will sail her back to Dun Laoghaire. Brud Clare can complete the repairs."

Ovens looked at McGarr.

"Leona Horrigan will pay the bill, I'm sure. It's the least she can do for you."

While speeding down the short stretch of dual carriageway in Shankhill, the program of popular music McGarr had switched on was interrupted. An announcer came on with a bulletin that Minister for Justice Horrigan had resigned.

Ovens turned to the window and looked out at the rock walls and empty fields they were passing.